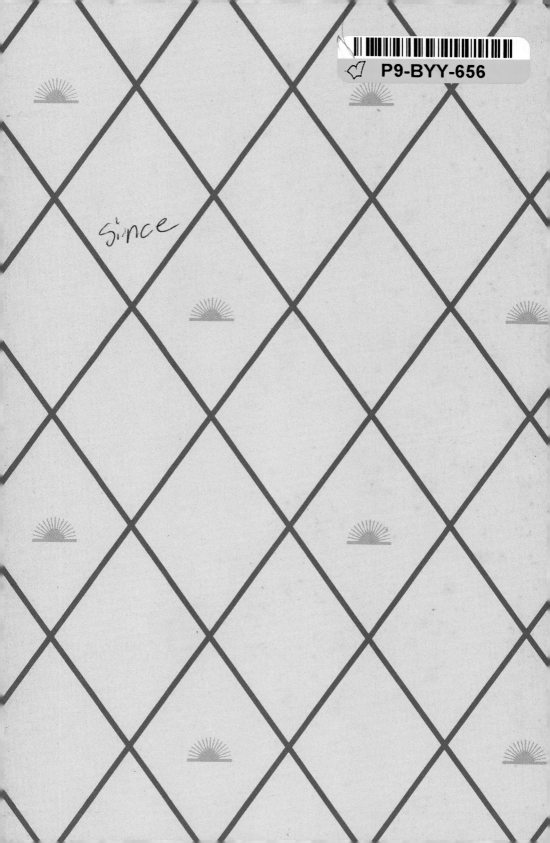

since

Reader's Digest

BEST LOVED BOOKS
FOR YOUNG READERS

Twenty Thousand Leagues Under the Sea

A CONDENSATION OF THE BOOK BY

Jules Verne

Illustrated by Hildibrand

CHOICE PUBLISHING, INC.
New York

PRODUCED IN ASSOCIATION WITH MEDIA PROJECTS INCORPORATED

Executive Editor, Carter Smith
Managing Editor, Jeanette Mall
Project Editor, Jacqueline Ogburn
Associate Editor, Charles Wills
Contributing Editor, Lise Brenner
Art Director, Bernard Schleifer

Library of Congress Catalog Number: 88-63349
ISBN: 0-945260-29-6

This 1989 edition is published and distributed by Choice Publishing, Inc.,
Great Neck, NY 11021, with permission of The Reader's Digest Association, Inc.

Manufactured in the United States of America.

10 9 8 7 6 5 4 3 2

Foreword

Twenty Thousand Leagues Under the Sea first appeared in 1870, when the idea of an underwater voyage around the world was conceivable only to scientists and crackpots. But the book captured the public imagination at once and has held it ever since; for even though some of Jules Verne's science may not stand up in the light of twentieth-century knowledge, the lonely figure of Captain Nemo and his prophetic *Nautilus* are still the stuff of romance.

Born in 1828 in the French seaport of Nantes, Verne grew up hearing strange tales of adventure on the high seas and in distant lands. In Paris studying law, he fell in with a circle of authors, including Alexandre Dumas, and soon began to write himself, shaping a new form of literature of his own invention—"science fiction." Before his death in 1905 he produced many books in this genre, including *The Mysterious Island, Voyage to the Center of the Earth*, and *Around the World in Eighty Days*.

Though he wrote about exciting subjects, Verne himself lived an uneventful life. He was, however, a meticulous researcher. Before writing *Twenty Thousand Leagues Under the Sea,* he not only read widely on maritime engineering and ocean life but also haunted the Paris aquarium to learn about exotic fish. He crossed the Atlantic on the *Great Eastern*, the world's first steam-propelled oceangoing city, studied its construction, and questioned its sailors extensively. In the United States he interviewed Cyrus Field, promoter of the Atlantic Cable.

Today Verne, who saw so clearly the shape of things to come, is known as the first real popularizer of the *romance* of science. More important, young people all over the world have read his novels, grown up, and proceeded to do the things about which he could only dream.

I. A SHIFTING REEF

EIGHTEEN SIXTY-SIX was marked by a strange occurrence, an amazing phenomenon that probably no one has yet forgotten. People living along the coasts, even people far inland, were disturbed by bizarre rumors. But seafaring men were especially upset. Merchants, sailors, skippers of Europe and America, naval officers of many nations, heads of state on both continents, all were deeply concerned.

Ships at sea had encountered "an enormous thing," a long, spindle-shaped object, sometimes phosphorescent, and infinitely larger and faster than any known sea animal such as a whale or other cetacean. The data entered in the logbooks of the various ships agreed in most respects as to the shape of the object or creature, the incalculable speed of its movements, its surprising power, and the peculiar life with which it seemed endowed. Classifying the mysterious apparition as a "fable" was out of the question.

On July 20, 1866, the steamer *Governor Higginson*, of the Calcutta and Burnach Company, met this moving mass five miles off the east coast of Australia. Captain Baker thought that he was in the presence of an unknown sandbank until, with a hissing sound, the object shot two columns of water a hundred and fifty feet into the air. Similar facts were noted on July 23, more than seven hundred nautical leagues* away, in the Pacific Ocean, by the *Columbus* of the West India Company. And fifteen days later, two thousand miles farther off, the *Helvetie* of the Compagnie Nationale and the *Shannon* of the Royal Mail Company were within sight of each other in the Atlantic when they *both* sighted the object! In an exchange of signals, they agreed that it must be over three hundred and fifty feet long.

Now the biggest whales that frequent the seas never exceed a hundred and eighty feet in length, if indeed they attain that, and these reports coming in one after the other all influenced public opinion. Thoughtless people joked about the phenomenon, and talk about a monster became the fashion in public places. They sang of it in the cafés, ridiculed it in the newspapers. Magazines ran caricatures of gigantic and imaginary creatures, from the white whale, the awful "Moby Dick," to the huge kraken, whose tentacles could pull down a five-hundred-ton ship.

At the same time an endless controversy between the credulous and the incredulous exploded in all the learned societies. Editors of scientific periodicals, quarreling with believers in the supernatural, spilled seas of ink. The cheaper periodicals, of course, joined in with zest. Finally an article in a well-known satirical journal settled the monster, giving it the deathblow amid a universal chorus of laughter. Wit had vanquished science, and the question seemed buried forever.

Early in 1867, however, new facts were brought before the public. Now it was no longer just a problem for scientists, it was a real menace for the world at large. "The question" took on a new form. The monster had become a small island, a rock, a reef maybe, but a reef of indefinite and shifting proportions!

On March 5, 1867, the *Moravian* of the Montreal Ocean Line, then in latitude 27° 30' and longitude 72° 15', struck on her starboard quarter a rock not marked on any chart. Had it not been for

---

*The league, a unit of measurement, varies from country to country and from time to time, but usually signifies a distance somewhere around three miles. When Verne uses "French leagues," he often states the equivalent in English miles. Other measures that it helps to know in reading Verne are: the fathom, six feet, and the cable, usually 100 fathoms, 600 feet, or the length of the standard nautical cable (in some navies, up to 720 feet).

the superior strength of her hull, the *Moravian* would have been broken by the shock and sunk with 237 passengers. The officers on deck at the time of the accident hurried aft. They could see nothing but a strong eddy about three cable lengths away, as if the surface had been violently agitated.

Even this grave event might have been forgotten, like so many others, if it had not been reenacted under similar circumstances. On April 13, 1867, the sea was beautiful, the breeze was good, and the *Scotia* of the reputable Cunard Line was going at thirteen and a half knots in longitude 15° 12' and latitude 45° 37'. At four seventeen p.m., while the passengers were enjoying lunch in the great salon, a slight shock was felt on the hull aft of the port paddle. The *Scotia* had not struck, she had *been* struck, apparently by something sharp and penetrating.

The shouts of the carpenter's watch, who rushed onto the bridge crying, "We're sinking! We're sinking!" frightened the passengers at first, but Captain Anderson hastened to reassure them. The *Scotia*, divided into seven compartments by strong bulkheads, could survive any leak. With members of the crew, Captain Anderson went down to ascertain the damage. He found a large hole, six feet in diameter, in the bottom of the fifth compartment. The sea was pouring in with great force. Such a leak could not be patched. The *Scotia* was obliged to return to Liverpool. There the engineers, inspecting the ship in dry dock, could scarcely believe their eyes: eight feet below the watermark was a regular rent, in the shape of an isosceles triangle! The break in the inch-and-a-half iron plates could not have been more neatly done by a punch. Obviously the instrument that had produced such a perforation was not of a common stamp!

And so once again public opinion was aroused. From this day on all casualties at sea that could not otherwise be accounted for were blamed on the "monster." No fewer than two hundred such unexplained losses were recorded at Lloyd's of London every year, and the "monster" was now accused of causing them all.

The public demanded that the sea be purged of this dread cetacean!

DURING THIS TIME, I had been working with a scientific research team in the Bad Lands of Nebraska, U.S.A. The French government had assigned me to that expedition in my capacity as assistant professor in the Paris Museum of Natural History. My return to France was scheduled for early June of 1867. I had arrived in New York, where I was classifying my botanical, mineralogical and zoological specimens, when the accident happened to the *Scotia*. The controversy was at its height during my stay in New York.

Of course, I was well up on the subject. I had read all the American and European papers without being any closer to an answer. The mystery fascinated me. The hypothesis of the floating island, the shifting reef, had been abandoned. Unless this shoal had a machine in its belly, how could it change position with such amazing speed? There remained only two possible solutions, and these created two distinct parties: on one side, those who believed in a monster of colossal strength; on the other side, those who believed in a submarine vessel of enormous power. Finding it impossible to form a solid opinion, I jumped from one extreme to the other.

The second hypothesis could not stand up against inquiries in both the Old World and the New. It was not likely that a private individual could have such a machine at his command. How could he have built it in secret? A government could perhaps possess such a destructive weapon, but the idea faded as one country after another issued formal denials. Since the public interest was at stake, and transatlantic commerce was suffering, their veracity could not be doubted. And indeed, how could the building of such a submarine boat have escaped the attention of professional spies?

Several people in New York did me the honor of asking for my opinion. In France I had published a two-volume work, *Mysteries of the Great Ocean Depths*, which had gained me a special reputation in this branch of natural history. "The Honorable Pierre Aronnax, Professor in the Museum of Paris," was called upon to give his views by, among others, the New York *Herald*. Here is an excerpt from my article that was run in the April 30 issue:

> After examining the different hypotheses one by one, we find it necessary to admit the existence of a marine animal of enormous power. The deepest parts of the ocean are unknown to us. What creatures can live twelve or fifteen miles down, we can hardly imagine. But let us face the dilemma. Either we know all the varieties of beings that inhabit our oceans, or we do not.
>
> If we do not know them all, nothing is more reasonable than to suppose the existence of fishes or cetaceans; or even of new species that have been living in the strata inaccessible to our soundings and that an accident of some sort has now brought up to the surface.
>
> If, on the other hand, we do know all living things, we must look for the animal among those marine beings already classified. In that case, I should be disposed to conceive of a gigantic narwhal. The common narwhal, or sea unicorn, often attains a length of twenty feet. It is armed with a kind of ivory sword, a halberd that has the hardness of steel. Increase the narwhal's size a dozen or more times, give it strength proportionate to that size, lengthen its destructive weapon, and you have the animal in question. It will have the proportions reported by the officers of the *Helvetie* and the *Shannon*, the power and the instrument needed to perforate the *Scotia*.
>
> Indeed, until I have better information, I shall assume such a sea unicorn to be the explanation of this mystery, unless there be something over and above all that one has ever conjectured, seen, or experienced; which is just within the realm of possibility.

Those last words were certainly cowardly. But I wanted to preserve my dignity as a professor and not give too much cause for Americans to laugh—they laugh hard when they do laugh. I reserved for myself a way out! In effect, though, I had admitted the existence of the "monster." My article was hotly discussed, and gained quite a reputation.

The United States was first to take action. In New York, a frigate of high speed, the *Abraham Lincoln*, under Commander Farragut, was commissioned to pursue the gigantic narwhal. But then for two months no one heard anything further about the monster. It seemed as if the unicorn knew of the conspiracy against it. It had been so much talked of, even over the Atlantic Cable, that jesters pretended the sly thing had stopped a telegram on its way. During this time no one knew what course to pursue. Impatience grew until, on June 2, it was learned that a steamer of the San Francisco Line had sighted the animal in the North Pacific.

The *Abraham Lincoln* was revictualed and well supplied with coal. Three hours before it left its Brooklyn pier I received this letter:

M. Aronnax, Fifth Avenue Hotel, New York
Sir: If you will consent to join the *Abraham Lincoln* on its expedition, the government of the United States will be pleased to see France represented in this enterprise. Commander Farragut has a cabin ready for you.

Cordially yours,
J. B. Hobson, Secretary of the Navy

Three seconds before receiving Hobson's letter, I had no more thought of chasing the unicorn than of finding the Northwest Passage. Three seconds after reading the letter, I felt that my true vocation in life was to pursue this monster and rid the sea of it.

Although after my exhausting expedition I wanted only to see my country, my friends, and my modest quarters near the Jardin des Plantes in Paris, I accepted the American invitation without hesitation. Besides, I told myself, all roads lead back to Europe, and the unicorn may be thoughtful enough to allow itself to be caught near the coast of France (for my special benefit), and I will bring back not less than two feet of its ivory spur for the Museum of Natural History.

"Conseil," I called impatiently.

Conseil was my servant, a faithful Flemish boy who had accompanied me for ten years on all my travels. I liked him, and he liked me. He was phlegmatic in temperament, rarely disturbed or even surprised, and quick and apt at any service required of him. Despite his name, he never gave *counsel*, even when asked for it. Never once had he complained, whether science had led us to China or the Congo. This boy was thirty years of age, and his age to that of his master was as fifteen to twenty. (May I be forgiven for this round-about way of admitting that I was forty?) But Conseil had one fault. He was ceremonious to the nth degree. He would never speak to me except in the third person, which was irksome at times.

"Conseil!" I was feverishly preparing to take off.

As a rule, I never asked him whether it was convenient for him to go along with me. But this time the expedition might be long and the enterprise hazardous. What would Conseil say?

He appeared. "Did monsieur call me?"

"Yes, my boy. Get ready. We leave in two hours."

"Whatever monsieur wishes," he answered quietly.

"Not a second to lose! Pack everything in my trunk—traveling kit, suits, shirts, socks—and hurry."

"And monsieur's latest collections?"

"I'll have them sent to France."

"Then *we* are not returning to Paris?" asked Conseil.

"Oh, yes," I answered evasively, "but by a detour."

"Whatever route monsieur prefers."

"Oh, it will be nothing at all; not quite so direct a route, that's all. We sail via the Pacific on the *Abraham Lincoln*."

"Whatever monsieur thinks proper," Conseil replied.

"You see, my friend, we're going to get rid of that famous monster! The author of a two-volume work on *Mysteries of the Great Ocean Depths* can't pass up a chance to go with Commander Farragut. A glorious mission, but give it a little thought! Maybe not everybody will come back."

"Whatever pleases monsieur."

He had our bags packed in fifteen minutes. In the lobby I paid our bill and gave instructions for sending my specimens to Paris. Soon Conseil and I were at the Brooklyn wharf where the *Abraham Lincoln* was belching black smoke from her two funnels.

Our luggage was carried to the deck of the frigate. A sailor led me to the poop, where a good-looking officer held out his hand to me. "Monsieur Pierre Aronnax?"

"Himself. Commander Farragut?"

"In person. You are welcome, Professor. Your cabin is ready."

The *Abraham Lincoln* was well equipped for her mission. Fitted with high-pressure engines, she could attain a speed of eighteen and a third knots. The ship's interior corresponded to her nautical qualities. I was pleased with my cabin. "We'll be comfortable here," I said to Conseil.

"As comfortable, if monsieur will permit me to say it, as a hermit crab in the shell of a whelk."

I left him to stow away our luggage and returned to the deck. Captain Farragut was ordering the men to cast loose the last moorings. The piers of Brooklyn, and all of New York bordering on the East River, were crowded. Three cheers burst from five hundred thousand throats as the *Abraham Lincoln* majestically entered the river, where she was surrounded by scores of ferryboats and small boats loaded with spectators. Then, following the New Jersey coast, she passed by the forts, which saluted her with their heavy guns. She answered by hoisting the American colors three times. Thirty-seven stars shone from the mizzen peak. An escort of boats and tenders still followed, not leaving her till they came abreast of the lightship which marks the entrance to New York Harbor.

The frigate skirted the Long Island coast. At eight in the evening, after having lost sight of the lights on Fire Island, we ran at full steam into the dark waters of the Atlantic.

III. AHOY! THE THING ITSELF!

COMMANDER FARRAGUT was an accomplished mariner. His frigate and he were one. On the question of the sea unicorn there was no doubt in his mind. He would allow no one on board to question its existence. The monster lived, and he had sworn to rid the seas of it. Either Farragut would kill the narwhal or the narwhal would kill Farragut. No third possibility!

Officers on board shared their captain's views. They were always calculating the chances of an encounter, watching intently the vast surface of the sea. The common sailors were too impatient to stay on deck; so long as the sun was in the sky, they were up in the rigging. The *Abraham Lincoln* had not yet breasted the waters of the Pacific, but Captain Farragut had mentioned a certain two thousand dollars, set aside for whoever should first sight the monster. I leave it to you to imagine how intently we all kept watch. Only Conseil seemed to be indifferent and out of keeping with the general enthusiasm.

As I have mentioned, Captain Farragut's ship had been equipped for catching a giant narwhal. No whaler had ever been better armed. We possessed every known device, from the harpoon thrown by hand to the blunderbuss with its barbed arrows and the duck gun with its explosive balls. On the forecastle was mounted the perfect breech-loading cannon—a model of which was on display at the Exhibition of 1867—that could throw a nine-pound projectile ten miles. And, best of all, the *Abraham Lincoln* had on board Ned Land, prince of harpooners.

Ned was a French Canadian. He came from a hardy family of Quebec fishermen. He was about forty, over six feet tall, strongly built, grave and taciturn, sometimes violent, and very bad tempered when contradicted. His physique attracted attention, but above all so did the boldness of his look.

As uncommunicative as Ned was, he took a liking to me. My nationality gave a chance for him to talk, and for me to hear that old language of Rabelais still in use in some of the French-Canadian provinces. He recounted his adventures to me, his fishing, his combats, in a naturally poetic manner. But what did he think about the monster? To tell the truth, he was the only one on board who did not believe in the unicorn. He even avoided the subject.

One magnificent evening, about three weeks after our departure, the frigate was abreast of Cape Blanc, thirty miles to leeward of the coast of Patagonia. Within a week we expected to enter the Pacific Ocean. Seated on the poop, Ned Land and I chatted of this and that as we looked out over the mysterious waters. I naturally led the talk to the giant narwhal.

"Ned, is it possible you have any reasons for doubting this creature's existence?"

The harpooner regarded me thoughtfully, striking his broad

9

forehead with his hand as if to collect himself, and said finally, "Maybe I do, Monsieur Aronnax."

"But Ned, you're a whaler by profession. You can easily accept the idea of enormous cetaceans. You should be the last to doubt!"

"That's just what deceives you, Professor. The common man believes in antediluvian monsters in the heart of the earth, but geologists don't. As a whaler, I've harpooned many a cetacean. And however strong and well armed they may have been, they could never have scratched the iron plates of a steamship."

"Ned, I've heard of ships that had been pierced by the tusk of the narwhal."

"Wooden ships, maybe," said the Canadian. "But I've never seen it done. And until I have further proof, I shall doubt that they can produce the effect you describe."

"Ned, I say this with a conviction based on the logic of the evidence. I believe in a mammal very powerfully organized, belonging to the vertebrates, like the whales and dolphins, and furnished with a spur of great penetrating power!"

"Ummmhhh." The harpooner shook his head, unconvinced.

"Look at it this way, my worthy Canadian. If such an animal exists miles below the surface of the sea, it must of necessity possess a constitution the strength of which would defy comparison."

"And why this powerful constitution?"

"Because it would need it to resist the pressure in those strata. Listen, Ned. The pressure of the atmosphere can be represented by the weight of a column of water thirty-two feet high. Right? Actually the column of water would be shorter, because we are talking of seawater, which is denser than fresh water. So, when you dive, Ned, your body bears a pressure equal to that of the atmosphere multiplied by as many times thirty-two feet of water as there are above you. That is to say, at three hundred and twenty feet the pressure equals ten times that of the atmosphere, at thirty-two hundred feet one hundred times that of the atmosphere, and so on. Now, my brave Ned, the pressure of the atmosphere itself is about fifteen pounds for every square inch of your body. Do you know how many square inches there are on the surface of your body?"

"I haven't the slightest idea, monsieur."

"About twenty-six hundred. At about fifteen pounds to the square inch, your twenty-six hundred square inches carry at this moment a pressure of . . . thirty-nine thousand pounds."

"Without my noticing it?"

"Without your noticing it. You are not crushed or even discomforted by such a pressure, because the air, the atmosphere itself, penetrates the interior of your body with equal pressure. But in the water it's a different matter."

"Yes, I can see that." Ned was becoming more interested. "The water surrounds me, but does not penetrate me."

"Exactly. At three hundred and twenty feet beneath the surface, the pressure equals ten times thirty-nine thousand pounds; at thirty-two hundred feet, a hundred times that, or three million, nine hundred thousand pounds; and at thirty-two thousand feet, or about six miles down, thirty-nine million pounds. You would be flattened as if by the plates of a hydraulic press!"

"The devil!" exclaimed Ned.

"So, my worthy harpooner, if a vertebrate several hundred yards long, with millions of square inches on the surface of its body, can maintain itself at such depths, imagine how strong its bone structure must be, how strong its constitution must be, to withstand a pressure of billions and billions of pounds!"

"Why," Ned said, "it would have to be made of iron plates eight inches thick, like the armored frigates."

"Right. And think what damage such a mass could inflict if hurled with the speed of an express train against a ship's hull."

"Yes . . . right . . . maybe." He was shaken by these figures but not yet willing to give in.

"Have I convinced you, Ned?"

"You've convinced me of one thing, Professor. If such animals do exist, they must be as strong as you say they are."

I didn't push my advantage. I would prove it, after we had captured the monster. But, day after day, the voyage of the *Abraham Lincoln* proved uneventful. The monotony was broken by just one memorable incident on June 30, when the frigate met some American whalers off the Falkland Islands. They had heard nothing new about the narwhal. But the captain of one of them, knowing that Ned Land had signed on board the *Abraham Lincoln*, asked for his help in chasing a whale they had sighted. Commander Farragut welcomed a chance to see Ned at work. Instead of one whale, our Canadian harpooned two with wondrous dexterity. I decided that if the monster ever met Ned, I would not bet on the monster.

With great speed, the frigate skirted the southeast coast of America. July 3 we were at the opening of the Strait of Magellan, but Commander Farragut decided to round Cape Horn itself. After all, it was highly unlikely that we would meet the narwhal in the narrow strait! As a number of sailors said, "He's much too big for that!" On July 8 the screw of the *Abraham Lincoln* was churning the waters of the Pacific. "Keep your eyes open!" the sailors cried.

And they were kept open. Eyes and glasses—a bit dazzled, it's true, by the prospect of two thousand dollars—had not a moment's rest. Even I, for whom money has little charm, was constantly on the alert. Eating quick snacks, taking only short naps, I did not leave the poop. How often I shared the frustrations of the men when some capricious whale raised its black back above the waves! In a moment the deck would be crowded, a moment later the simple creature would disappear amid a hail of curses. Still I looked, while Conseil, always phlegmatic, would repeat: "If monsieur would not stare so much, he would see better." Ned, however, remained indifferent, refusing to scan the sea except when he was officially on duty. I had to agree with him that our chances of spotting this creature—"If it really exists," as he pointed out—were becoming very slight.

On July 20 we cut the Tropic of Capricorn, and seven days later we crossed the equator on the 110th meridian. Now the frigate took a western course and scoured the central waters of the Pacific. Captain Farragut felt that it was better to stay in deep waters, and keep clear of continents and islands, which the beast itself seemed to avoid. We passed at some distance from the Marquesas and the Sandwich Islands, crossed the Tropic of Cancer, and made for the China seas. Now we were in the area where the monster had last been reported, and, truly, the entire crew underwent a nervous excitement which I can hardly describe: they would not eat; they would not sleep; twenty times a day a misinterpretation or an optical illusion would get us all into a deep sweat. Our emotions were so violent that a reaction was inevitable.

And the reaction did set in, mounting from crew to officers. For three months, during which every day was an age, the *Abraham Lincoln* had plowed the waters of the North Pacific. The most enthusiastic supporters of the project now became its warmest enemies. This useless search could not go on. The crew of the *Abraham Lincoln* had done their best. Their failure was not their fault; there was nothing to do but go home. I will not say there was mutiny; but after a reasonable period of obstinacy, Captain Farragut (like Columbus before him!) asked his dissatisfied crew for just three days more. If in three days they did not sight the monster, the *Abraham Lincoln* would make for the Atlantic.

He made this promise on November 3. Actually it had the effect of rallying the crew, who watched the ocean with renewed interest. Each man wanted one last look with which to sum up his remembrance.

Two days passed; the steam was at half pressure; we tried a thousand schemes to attract the animal. We trailed large quantities of bacon in our wake, to the great satisfaction of the sharks. Small craft radiated in all directions from the *Abraham Lincoln* as she lay to. But the night of November 5 arrived with the mystery still unsolved. Next day, the delay would expire.

We were then in latitude 31° 15' north and longitude 136° 42' east. The coast of Japan was less than two hundred miles to leeward. Night was coming on. They had just struck eight bells; large clouds covered the face of the moon. The sea undulated peacefully under the bow. I was leaning over the starboard rail. The crew, perched in the ratlines, studied the horizon, which darkened little by little. Officers scoured the growing dark with their night glasses. Sometimes the ocean sparkled with the rays of the moon, which darted between clouds. Then all traces of light were gone.

Looking at Conseil, standing next to me, I imagined he was feeling, for a change, a bit of the general excitement. "Come, Conseil, this is your last chance at the two thousand dollars."

"May I be permitted to say, sir, that I never reckoned on getting the prize, and had the United States government offered a hundred thousand, they would have been none the poorer."

"I think you're right, Conseil. It was a foolish, rash thing to get involved in. How much time we've lost! We could have been back in France six months ago."

"In monsieur's museum!" he added. "By now I would have classified all of monsieur's fossils."

"Yes, you're right, Conseil. I guess we'll be laughed at for our troubles, too."

"That's tolerably certain," he answered quietly. "I think they will make fun of the professor. And—"

He didn't have time to finish his sentence. In the midst of the silence all around us a voice had just rung out. It was Ned Land, shouting: "Ahoy! The thing itself! Abeam to leeward!"

At this cry, the entire crew hurried toward the harpooner. Engineers left their engines, stokers their furnaces.

Commander Farragut had given the order to stop, and the frigate was drifting. The darkness was profound. However, two cable lengths from the frigate, on the starboard quarter, the ocean seemed to be illuminated from below! The monster itself was emerging from the water, throwing out that intense light mentioned in the reports of several captains.

"That's only a mass of phosphorescent organisms," one lieutenant said.

"No sir, certainly not," I answered. "That brightness is *electric* in nature! Besides, look! It's darting straight toward us!"

A chorus of cries rose from the frigate.

"Silence!" shouted the captain. "Helm alee, reverse engines!" The crew returned to their stations. Beating to port, the *Abraham Lincoln* described a semicircle. "Right helm! Go ahead!"

We tried to sheer off, but the supernatural beast approached with a velocity double our own!

Amazement more than fear made us speechless and motionless. The animal gained on us, sporting with the waves. It circled the frigate, which was then making fourteen knots, and enveloped us with its electric rings! Then it would move away two or three miles, leaving a phosphorescent track, like the steam of an express train. Then all at once, from the dark horizon, it would rush toward us again with alarming speed, stopping suddenly about twenty feet from our hull, dying down as if the source of illumination were exhausted. Then it would appear on the other side of the frigate, as if it had turned over and slid under our hull. Any second a collision could have occurred which would have been fatal—to us. And I was astonished at the maneuvers of the frigate. She did not fight, she fled. I expressed my amazement to the captain. His usually impassive look had changed to one of bewilderment.

"Monsieur Aronnax," he said, "I will not risk my frigate in this darkness with such a creature. Wait for daylight; the situation will change."

"You have no doubt, Captain, of the nature of the monster?"

"No, Professor. It is a gigantic narwhal, an electric one. It must be the most terrible animal ever created."

No one thought of sleeping that night. The *Abraham Lincoln*, incapable of competing with such velocity, sailed at half speed. The narwhal, imitating the frigate, was just riding the waves. Toward midnight, though, it disappeared, or, to use a better expression, it just "died out" like a large glowworm. Had it fled? But at twelve fifty-three a.m. we heard a deafening whistle like that produced by water rushing violently.

Captain Farragut, Ned and I were on the poop, peering through the darkness. "Ned Land," the commander asked, "you've often heard whales roar?"

"Very often, Captain! If I could just get within four harpoon lengths . . ."

"But for that I would have to put a whaleboat at your disposal," the captain said. "And that would be risking the lives of my men."

"Mine too," the harpooner added.

Toward two a.m. the great light reappeared, about five miles to windward. In spite of the distance we could hear the strokes of the beast's tail, even its panting breath. It seemed that when it surfaced to take breath, air was sucked into its lungs like steam sucked into the vast cylinders of a two-thousand-horsepower engine.

A whale, I thought, with the strength of a cavalry regiment!

All night we were on the alert. Day began to break at six o'clock, and then the narwhal's electric light went out. But by seven a thick fog obscured our view; the best spyglasses could not pierce it. The men were disappointed, even angry. I climbed the mizzenmast; some officers were already perched on the mastheads. By eight o'clock the fog began to rise in thick scrolls. The horizon grew clearer. Suddenly, just as on the preceding day, we heard Ned Land's voice: "The thing itself, on the port quarter!"

Every eye looked where he pointed. There, a mile and a half away, a long black body emerged a yard above the surface. Never did a fishtail beat the water with such violence. An immense white track described the animal's course. As we approached the animal, I studied it carefully.

The captains of the *Shannon* and the *Helvetie* had exaggerated its size. I estimated its length as only two hundred and fifty feet. As I watched, two jets of steam and water shot from its vents and rose a hundred and twenty feet into the air, and so I ascertained its method of breathing. I concluded definitely that it belonged to the vertebrates, class of mammals, division of pisciforms, order of cetaceans, family of . . . But that I could not tell. The cetaceans comprise three families: whales, porpoises, dolphins. If this was a narwhal, then it would be classified with the dolphins.

The commander called the engineer: "Stoke your fires and full speed ahead!"

Three cheers greeted this command. The time for battle had arrived. Moments later the frigate's two funnels vomited forth torrents of black smoke, the bridge quaked with the trembling of the boilers, and the *Abraham Lincoln* made straight for the monster. The beast allowed us to come within half a cable length. Then, disdaining to dive, it swerved a bit, slowed down and swerved again.

For three quarters of an hour we chased the monster without gaining two feet on it. In a rage, the commander tugged at his thick beard. "Mr. Land, do you think I should put out the boats?" he asked.

"No sir," Ned replied. "We can't take that beast so easily. But put on more steam, sir, if you can. With your permission, I'll post myself under the bowsprit. If we get close enough, I'll harpoon it!"

"Go ahead, Ned. Engineer, more pressure!"

Ned went to the bowsprit. The fires were built up, the screw was revolving forty-three times a minute, the steam was shooting out of the valves. Heaving the log, we calculated that the *Abraham Lincoln* was making eighteen and a half knots.

But the monster was also going at a speed of eighteen and a half knots!

We kept up this pace for another hour without gaining a foot. It was humiliating for one of the swiftest men-of-war in the United States Navy. The captain no longer tugged at his beard; he chewed it. He called the engineer again. "Have you reached maximum pressure?"

"Yes sir! The valves are charged at six and one half atmospheres."

"Charge them at ten atmospheres!"

There was a typical Yankee command! Do the impossible! I felt as if we were engaged in one of those fabulous steamboat races on the Mississippi River. "Conseil," I said to my servant, "you realize that we'll all be blown up when the boiler bursts?"

"Whatever monsieur wishes," he answered.

The *Abraham Lincoln*'s speed increased. Her masts trembled right down into the stepping holes. They heaved the log again. "Nineteen and three-tenths knots, sir."

"Clap on more steam!"

Now the pressure gauge showed ten atmospheres! But the cetacean was getting up steam too. Ned Land kept to his post, harpoon in hand for the few times the animal let us gain a bit.

"Now we'll get it!" the Canadian would cry. But just as he was poised to strike, the cetacean would steal away with a speed of at least thirty knots. Even during our top speed the monster would bully the frigate, going round and round her. Cries of fury broke from the crew.

By noon we had made absolutely no progress. The captain decided to take extreme measures. "We'll see whether that animal can move faster than shells! Mate, send your men to the forecastle!"

They loaded the forecastle gun, and their first shot passed over the cetacean, which was half a mile away.

"Somebody with better aim!" the captain ordered. "Five hundred dollars to whoever hits that infernal monster!"

An old gunner with a gray beard and steady eye—I can see him yet—stepped up to the gun and took aim. A loud *boom* was followed by cheers from the crew. It was a hit! But the shell only glanced off the animal's rounded surface and splashed into the sea.

"That's enough!" the old cannoneer shouted in a rage. "That thing is covered with armor plate!"

The captain cursed. As we renewed the chase, he leaned toward me and said, "I will pursue that beast until my ship blows up!"

"Yes," I answered, "and you are right to risk it!"

But how I wished that the monster would exhaust itself! Hour after hour, it showed no signs of weariness.

As night came on, overshadowing a rough sea, I reckoned that the *Abraham Lincoln* had traveled at least three hundred miles during this unlucky day. I thought that now our expedition was over we would never see this extraordinary animal again. But I was wrong. At ten fifty p.m. the electric light reappeared three miles to windward, as bright as the night before. The narwhal seemed motionless though. Perhaps it slept at last, floating with the undulations of the sea. Here was a chance that Captain Farragut would not miss!

He gave the orders. Ned returned to his post under the bowsprit, and at half steam the frigate advanced cautiously so as not to waken its adversary. It is not unusual in the ocean to meet whales so sound asleep that they can be attacked successfully. Noiselessly we approached. Deep silence reigned on the bridge. Leaning on the forecastle rail, I could see Ned below me. When we were twenty feet from the sleeping monster, he grasped the martingale in one hand and brandished his harpoon with the other. Suddenly his arm straightened. The harpoon shot out. I heard a deep, ringing stroke, as though his weapon had collided with a hard surface.

The electric light died out. Two enormous waterspouts broke over the frigate, flooding us from stem to stern, knocking men down. I felt a dreadful shock. Unable to stop myself, I was flung over the rail. I tumbled far out into the waves.

IV. CHANGING WITH CHANGE

I SANK TO A DEPTH of about twenty feet, but I'm a pretty good swimmer and I was able to keep my head. With two kicks I reached the surface. My first thought was the frigate. Had the crew seen me go overboard? Could I hope to be rescued?

Through the intense dark I could see her lights fading into the distance. I was lost!

"Help!" In desperation I swam after the ship. My clothes seemed glued to my skin, paralyzing my movements. My mouth filled with water, and I struggled against being pulled down.

Suddenly I felt myself grasped by a firm hand, and heard these words pronounced close to my ear: "If monsieur would just lean on my shoulder, monsieur would be able to swim more easily."

With one hand I seized my faithful Conseil's arm. "You!" I said. "You were thrown overboard too?"

"No, but being monsieur's servant, I followed him."

"And the frigate?"

"I think"—he turned on his back—"that monsieur had better not rely on the frigate."

"Why?"

"When I jumped overboard, I heard someone at the wheel saying that the propeller and the rudder were broken by the monster's tusk. That's all that happened to her. But for us that's enough—she can't answer her helm. Still, we can last several hours yet, and a lot can happen in that time."

His coolness gave me strength. I tried swimming more vigorously, but my clothes hampered me.

"Will monsieur allow me?" Conseil slipped an open knife under my clothes, slitting them from top to bottom. He pulled them off me while I swam for both of us. Then I did the same for him, and we swam more easily, staying close together.

We agreed that, since our only hope lay in being picked up by the frigate's boats, we ought to try to wait for them as long as possible. That meant saving our strength. And this is how we did it. One of us would lie on his back, with arms crossed, legs outstretched, and the other would swim and push him ahead. Relieving each other every ten minutes or so, we could swim on for hours, perhaps even until daylight. Slight chance! But hope is so firmly rooted in the heart of man, I doubt we could have killed it if we had wanted to.

The sea was very calm. The deep darkness was broken only by the phosphorescence caused by our swimming. I watched the luminous waves moving over my hand; it seemed as if we were in a bath of mercury.

In a few hours I was exhausted, my limbs stiffened with violent cramps. Conseil kept me afloat. Our survival depended on him alone. I could hear him panting. I did not think he could last much longer.

"Leave me, Conseil! Save yourself!"

"Abandon monsieur? I would rather drown first."

At that moment the moon emerged from the edge of a cloud, and the sea glistened with its rays. Looking around the horizon, I discovered the frigate! She was about five miles off, barely perceptible. There were no boats in sight! I wanted to shout. But what good would it do, at that distance? My swollen lips could produce no sounds. But I heard Conseil shouting at intervals, "Help! Help!"

We stopped swimming to see if . . . I thought I heard an answer, or was that just the ringing in my ears? "Did you hear something?"

"Yes, yes!" And Conseil called out once more.

This time there could be no mistake. A human voice responded!

Leaning on my shoulder, Conseil raised himself half out of the water. He fell back panting.

"What did you see?"

"I saw . . ." he murmured, "saw . . . but don't talk . . . save . . . strength. . . ."

What had he seen? The thought of the monster occurred to me! But that voice?

Conseil was pushing me again. Sometimes he raised his head, said something, and was answered by a voice that came nearer each time. But I could scarcely hear. My strength was waning, my mouth filling with brine. I was numb with cold. I raised my head once and sank. Then I hit some hard body. Roused, I clung to it, felt that I was being raised, that I was brought to the surface, that my chest collapsed. I fainted.

I came to because someone was rubbing me vigorously. I half opened my eyes. "Conseil," I murmured.

"Did monsieur call me?" Conseil answered.

At that moment, by the light of the moon, which was sinking toward the horizon, I saw a face that was not Conseil's. "Ned!" I cried.

"In person, Professor. And after my prize!"

"Were you thrown overboard too by the collision?"

"Yes, Professor, but I was luckier than you. I landed on a floating island or, to be more accurate, on our gigantic narwhal. And I found out why my harpoon had not pierced its skin!"

"Please explain, Ned. Why?"

"Because this beast, Professor, is made of sheet iron."

The Canadian's last words stirred up a revolution in my brain. I wriggled my way up to the summit of this half-submerged being or object which was serving as our refuge and kicked it. It was hard and impenetrable, not the soft substance that covers great marine mammals. Still, it could be a bony carapace, like that of the antediluvian animals. I could class this monster among the amphibious reptiles. But no! The blackish back on which I was sitting was unquestionably metallic. My kicks produced a metallic sound. There could be no doubt—it was made of riveted plates! This monster that had intrigued the world of science, and confused the imagination of seamen from two hemispheres, was an even more astonishing phenomenon—a man-made thing shaped like an immense steel fish.

"I've been on it for three hours," Ned said, "and it hasn't stirred."

"But it must have machinery," I concluded, "and machinery requires mechanics so—we're saved!"

"Hunh." Ned sounded skeptical.

At that moment a bubbling commenced at the rear end of this strange thing, and we began to move. We barely had time to get hold of the topside, which rose about a yard out of the water.

"So long as it sails horizontally," Ned muttered, "I don't mind so much. But if it takes a fancy to plunge, I would not give two dollars for my hide!"

It was clearly necessary to communicate with the beings, whatever they were, inside this machine. I searched all over the outside for an opening, but the iron plates were joined tight with rows and rows of rivets. Then the moon disappeared and left us in darkness, and suddenly the machine increased its speed. Now, with the waves beating against us, we found it much harder to hang on. Fortunately, Ned located a mooring ring, and we held tight.

Further memories of this long night are vague, but day came at last. I was about to resume my examination of the hull when I felt the whole thing sinking bit by bit.

"Oh, the devil!" Ned kicked the resounding plates. "Open up, you ornery . . ."

Fortunately the sinking ceased. Suddenly noises, as of iron parts being pushed aside, came from within. An iron plate was raised. A man appeared, uttered a strange cry and disappeared. Moments later, eight strapping fellows, with faces masked, came out and dragged us down into their formidable machine.

As THE HATCH CLOSED OVER ME, I was enveloped in profound darkness. I felt my naked feet touching the rungs of an iron ladder. Ned and Conseil were following me. At the bottom of the ladder a door opened, then shut behind us with a bang.

We seemed to be alone. Where? I could not imagine. Everything was black, thick black. I was trembling all over. Whom did we have to contend with? Pirates?

Ned gave free vent to his indignation. "A thousand devils! These people match the Scotch for hospitality! I bet they're cannibals! But they won't eat me without a fight first!"

"Calm yourself, friend Ned," Conseil said gently. "We are not quite done for yet."

"Not quite," the Canadian said sharply, "but things certainly look black! Fortunately, I still have my bowie knife, and I can use that even in the dark!"

"Please, Ned, do not lose your self-control," I said. "Do not compromise us with useless violence. How do you know they will not listen to us? Now let us try to find out where we are."

Taking five steps, I came to an iron wall. Turning back, I struck a table, against which were placed several stools. The floor was covered with a thick mat. Another bare wall gave no sign of window or door. Conseil, going around the other way, bumped into me, and together we returned to the middle of the room, which, I estimated, measured about twenty feet by ten. As to its height, Ned, in spite of his great stature, could not reach the ceiling.

Half an hour passed without our situation changing when suddenly our prison was lighted so strongly that I could not bear it at first. I recognized the whiteness and intensity of the electric light that had played around the monster with such magnificent phosphorescence. First I shut my eyes involuntarily; then I opened them to see that this illumination came from a frosted half globe set in the ceiling.

"At last we can see," cried Ned, bowie knife in hand.

"Yes," I said, "but we're still in the dark about ourselves."

Suddenly we heard a noise of bolts, a door opened, and two men entered. They wore caps made of sea-otter fur, boots of sealskin, and loose-fitting garments made of an unrecognizable material. The first was short and muscular, with an abundance of black hair on his strong head, a thick mustache, and a penetrating look. His whole personality was stamped with the vivacity that we usually associate with the people of Provence.

The second, apparently the commander, deserves a more detailed description. Without hesitation, I could tell his dominant qualities: self-confidence, because his head was well set on his shoulders, and his black eyes looked around with assurance; calmness, because his skin, rather pale, showed coolness of blood; energy, because of the rapid contraction of his lofty brows; and courage, because his deep breathing indicated great lung power. But whether he was thirty-five or fifty I could not tell. He was tall, had a large forehead, straight nose, a clearly defined mouth, fine tapered hands. This was certainly the most admirable specimen of manhood I had ever seen. One outstanding feature was his eyes, rather far from each other, which—I verified this later—could take in nearly a quarter of the horizon at once. Yet, when he fixed on us, his large eyelids closed around so as to contract the range of his vision, and he looked as if he magnified us.

After he had studied us thus, he turned and talked with his companion in a strange tongue. It was a sonorous, harmonious language, with a great variety of vowel sounds.

The other replied with a shake of the head and a few incomprehensible words. Then he seemed to question me with a stare.

I responded by saying, in my best French, that I did not know his language, but he seemed not to understand.

"If monsieur were to tell our story," Conseil said, "perhaps these gentlemen could make out the key words."

I announced our names and occupations, and then recounted our adventures, articulating each syllable clearly. The tall man listened politely, but nothing in his face showed that he understood my story. When I concluded he said nothing.

There was another chance—English. Perhaps they would know this almost universal language. I knew it, as I knew German, well enough to read fluently but not well enough to speak correctly. "Ned, it's your turn. Speak your best Anglo-Saxon, and try to do better than I have."

Ned recommenced our story, in English. To my factual account he added some emotional questions. What did they mean, locking us up? Hadn't they ever heard of habeas corpus? To his disgust, he was no more successful than I. Our visitors did not stir. Having exhausted our linguistic resources, I had no idea what to do next, when Conseil said, "With monsieur's permission, I will explain in German."

I was amazed to hear that he knew the language; he protested that most Belgians do. But in spite of his elegant turns of phrase, Conseil failed too. At last, nonplussed, I tried to remember my first lessons and to narrate our adventures in Latin, but with no greater success. The two strangers exchanged a few words in their strange tongue and left. The door shut.

"This is infamous!" Ned Land broke out. "We'll die of hunger in this iron cage!"

"Bah," Conseil said, "we can hold out for some time yet."

"We must not despair, my friends," I said. "We have been worse off than this. Do me the favor of waiting before you form an opinion of the commander and his crew."

"My opinion is formed," Ned said sharply. "They are villains from the Land of Villains!"

"Brave Ned, that country is not clearly marked on the map of the world. But I admit that the nationality of the strangers is hard to figure out. I am inclined to think they have southern blood in their veins. I cannot decide by their appearance or talk whether they are Spaniards, Turks, Arabians or Indians."

"Now we are seeing the disadvantage of not having a universal language," said Conseil.

The door opened. A steward entered with shirts, coats and trousers made of the material I could not recognize. We dressed while the steward—dumb, perhaps deaf—set the table for three.

"This is more like it," said Conseil.

"Bah," said Ned, "what do you suppose they eat? Filleted shark, sea-dog steaks?"

"Let's find out," said Conseil.

Dishes of bell metal were placed on the table and we took our places. Doubtless we had civilized people to reckon with. Except for the electric light, I could have fancied I was in the dining room of the Grand-Hôtel in Paris. There was neither bread nor wine, but the water was fresh and clear. Among the dishes brought to us I recognized several fish delicately dressed; but other dishes I could not even identify as animal or vegetable. The dinner service was elegant and in perfect taste. Each plate and utensil had a letter engraved on it, with a motto arranged around it, a Latin phrase meaning "Changing with Change":

This motto applied perfectly to the submarine, which was mobile within a mobile element! And the letter N was doubtless the initial of the enigmatic commander.

Ned and Conseil were not meditating on such matters. They devoured the food. I felt reassured about our fate; it seemed clear our hosts would not let us die of hunger.

Our appetites appeased, we felt overcome with drowsiness. My companions stretched out on the carpet and were soon sound asleep. For my own part, too many thoughts crowded my head. Where were we? What strange power was propelling us? I fancied I felt the machine sinking to the lowest depths. Dreadful nightmares beset me. Then at last I grew calmer, my imagination dissolved into vague unconsciousness and I fell into deep slumber.

V. THE MAN OF THE SEAS

I HAD NO WAY of knowing exactly how long we had slept, but from my feeling of complete rest I knew we had slept for many hours. The first to wake, I found my companions still stretched out. Rousing myself, I studied our cell carefully. Nothing seemed changed, but during our slumbers the steward had cleared the table.

Now I realized that I was breathing with some difficulty. Although our cell was large, we had evidently consumed most of the oxygen it contained. It was becoming urgent to renew the atmosphere in our cell and, no doubt, in the entire ship. Now, I wondered, how does the commander do this? Does he purify the air chemically—this would require regular visits to shore to get the chemicals—or does he store air under pressure in tanks? Or—simply and economically, therefore most likely—does he just rise and take breath at the surface, like a cetacean? No matter what his method was, it seemed to me time to use it!

I was almost at the point of gasping for whatever oxygen still remained when I felt the boat rolling. Suddenly I was refreshed by a current of pure air, perfumed with salt, that came from a ventilator over the door. Evidently the iron-plated monster did rise to the surface to breathe, after the fashion of whales.

I was making these observations when Ned and Conseil awoke. They rubbed their eyes, stretched, then sprang to their feet.

"Has monsieur slept well?" asked Conseil.

"Very well, my brave boy. And you, Ned?"

"Soundly, Professor. But—do I smell a sea breeze?"

I told the Canadian all that had happened.

"Good!" he said. "That explains those roarings we heard when the *Abraham Lincoln* sighted the narwhal. But Professor, I have no idea what time it is, except that maybe it's dinnertime."

"Dinnertime, my friend? I'd say breakfast time. I think we have begun another day."

"Dinner or breakfast," Ned answered, "I'll welcome the steward, whichever he brings."

"Master Land," I said, "we must conform to the rules of the ship. If our appetites are ahead of the cook's clock . . ."

"Then we wait," said Conseil.

"That's just like you, Conseil," said Ned impatiently. "You would die of hunger rather than complain."

"What good would complaining do?" asked Conseil.

"Complaining doesn't have to *do* good, it *feels* good! If pirates lock me up, I'm going to sound off! Professor, what do you make of this?"

"I think we've blundered into somebody's big secret. If they need desperately to keep their secret secret, I don't think our lives are worth much. But promise me you'll make the best of things until we can size up the situation."

"Yeah, I promise. I won't show how I feel—even if I starve."

Yes, we were getting fearfully hungry, and still no steward. Ned got angrier and angrier. Notwithstanding his promise, I dreaded an explosion when he found himself with one of the crew.

For two hours more Land's temper increased. He shouted, but in vain. The iron walls were deaf. The silence was supernatural. The boat did not move, or I would have felt the trembling of the screw. Conseil stayed calm, I was getting terrified. Ned was roaring.

Just then the steward entered. Before I could stop him, the Canadian had thrown the man down and was holding him by the throat. I was going to intervene when suddenly I was nailed to the spot by hearing these words spoken in French: "Stop that, Master Land! And Professor! Will you be so kind as to listen to me?"

IT WAS THE COMMANDER.

Ned stood up. The captain motioned the choking steward out of the door. Then, leaning against the table, arms folded, he looked at us carefully. We waited for the outcome.

After several moments of silence, which none of us dared break, "Gentlemen," he said in a calm, penetrating tone, "I speak French, English, German, yes, even Latin. And so I could have answered you at our first interview. But I wanted to learn something about you first, and then to reflect on what I learned. Since your four separate accounts all agreed on the main points, I was convinced that you had properly identified yourselves. I know now that chance has brought to my ship Monsieur Pierre Aronnax, professor of natural history in the Paris Museum; Conseil, his servant; and Ned Land, harpooner on board the *Abraham Lincoln*."

I bowed agreement. He expressed himself with perfect ease, with not a trace of accent. Yet I did not *feel* that he was a Frenchman!

He went on: "I have waited a long time to pay you this second visit, but I wanted to consider very seriously how to act toward you. Through most annoying circumstances you have intruded on the life of a man who has broken all ties with humanity."

"Unintentionally!" I said.

"Unintentionally?" He raised his voice a bit. "Was it unintentionally that the *Abraham Lincoln* chased me all over the ocean? Unintentionally that your cannonballs bounced off my vessel and that Master Land struck me with his harpoon?"

There was a restrained irritation in his words. But I had an answer to these charges. "Sir, you are unaware of the public feeling in America and Europe that has been excited by reports from ships that have collided with your submarine boat. I ignore for now the numerous hypotheses by which men have attempted to explain this phenomenon to which you alone possess the secret. But you must understand that, in pursuing you, we on the *Abraham Lincoln* believed that we were chasing a sea monster that had to be destroyed at any cost."

A half smile curled his lips. "Do you dare affirm, Professor, that your frigate would not have pursued and cannonaded a submarine boat as readily as a monster?"

This embarrassed me. Surely Captain Farragut would not have hesitated.

"You see, then, that I have the right to treat you as enemies. Nothing obliges me to show you the least hospitality. I could place you on the deck of this vessel, I could submerge, and forget that you had ever bothered me. Wouldn't that be my right?"

"The right of a savage," I said. "Not the right of a civilized man."

"Professor, I am not what you call a civilized man. I am through with society, for reasons that I alone can appreciate. Therefore I don't obey its laws, and I suggest that you never again refer to them in my presence!"

That was plain talk. A flash of disdainful anger kindled in his eyes. I had a glimpse of a terrible past in this man's life. Not only had he put himself outside the pale of human laws, but also he had made himself independent of them, free in the strictest sense of the word! Who could pursue him to the bottom of the sea when he defied attacks on the surface? No man could demand from him an account of his actions. God, if he believed in Him—his conscience, if he had one—were the sole judges to whom he answered.

The commander continued to speak: "I have thought that my own interest might be reconciled with that pity to which every human being has some claim. You will stay on board my vessel, since fate has brought you here. You will be free. In exchange for this liberty, I shall impose only one condition. Your word of honor to accept it will suffice."

"I suppose, sir, this condition is one that a man of honor can accept?"

"Certainly. It is this. Certain unforeseeable events may at times force me to confine you to your cabins. Since I prefer never to use violence, I expect from you, more than from the others, a passive obedience. Acting in this way, I shall take full responsibility, for I shall make it impossible for you to see what ought not be seen. Do you accept?"

So things did take place on board that ought not to be seen by people still under the influence of society's laws.

"We accept," I said. "But I ask permission to address just one question to you."

"Yes?"

"You said we should be free on board. What do you mean by this liberty?"

"The freedom to come, to go, to see all that goes on, save under those rare conditions—the same liberty that my crew and I enjoy."

Clearly we did not understand each other. "Pardon me, sir, but this is the liberty that every prisoner has, the freedom to pace his cell. You mean we must give up country, friends, family?"

"Yes, Professor. But to renounce that worldly yoke that men call liberty is not so painful as you think."

"Never," said Ned, "will I give my word of honor not to try to escape."

"Master Land," the commander said coldly, "I did not ask you for your word of honor."

"Sir"—I was beginning to get angry—"you are taking advantage of us. This is cruelty."

"No, it is clemency. You are prisoners of war. I detain you alive although I could quite simply plunge you into the depths. You have stumbled on a secret—the secret of my whole existence. Do you think I can send you back to that world that must know nothing about my present life? Never! In detaining you, it is not you whom I guard. It is myself."

"You give us, then, simply the choice between life and death?"

"That's it."

"My friends"—I turned to Ned and Conseil—"faced with such alternatives, we have only one answer. But we are bound by no commitments to the master of this ship."

"None," said the commander. In a gentler tone he said, "Allow me to finish. I know of you, Professor Aronnax. You will not find life aboard this ship unbearable. You will find among my favorite books a copy of your two-volume work on the depths of the sea. I have read and reread it. You have carried your studies as far as *terrestrial* science can go. But you do not know all, because you have not seen all. Let me tell you, Professor, you will not regret the time spent on board—you are going to visit the land of marvels!"

I cannot deny it, those words had a great effect on me. For a moment I forgot that contemplation of these sublime phenomena was not worth the loss of my liberty. Besides, I trusted to the future to resolve the situation. I contented myself with saying, "By what name, what title should we address you?"

"To you, Professor," the commander replied, "I am nothing but Captain Nemo. You and your friends are nothing to me but passengers on the *Nautilus*." He called a steward and gave him orders in that strange language. Then, turning to Conseil and Ned, he said, "The table is set in your cabin. Please follow this man."

Ned and Conseil left the cell.

"And now, Professor, *our* meal is ready. Permit me to show you the way."

Passing through the door, I found myself in a passageway lighted by electricity, similar to the gangway of a more conventional ship. A dozen yards or so and a second door opened before me. I entered a dining room, decorated in perfect taste. High oaken sideboards, inlaid with ebony, stood at the two ends of the room. Their shelves contained porcelain and cut glass of great value. Silver sparkled in the light shed by the luminous ceiling. Exquisite paintings tempered and softened the glare.

A table was set in the center of the room. Captain Nemo pointed to my place. "You must be famished," he said.

The spread comprised many seafood dishes and many others unknown to me. But they were tasty. Captain Nemo was watching me. "Most of these dishes are absolutely new to you," he said, "but eat them without any anxiety. Since we have renounced the foods of the land, my crew and I are never ill."

"Do all these dishes come from the sea?"

"Yes, Professor. I tow my nets, and pull them in ready to break. Sometimes I hunt on the ocean floor, and stalk game in my submarine forests. I have vast properties on the immense prairies of the ocean, sown by the hand of the Creator and cultivated by me."

"Oh, I can understand that you are furnished with fish and other aquatic game. But how about this?" I pointed to slices of steak.

"This, which you take to be meat, Professor, is fillet of turtle. I never eat the flesh of land animals. Those, which you probably take to be stewed pork, are dolphins' livers. My cook is clever in preparing these marine products. Let me offer you some preserve of anemone, equal to that of the most delicious fruits. Here is sugar made of rockweed, and cream—made from whale's milk!"

I sampled and tasted, more out of curiosity than as a connoisseur.

"Professor, the ocean does more than just feed us. The cloth you're wearing is made from shellfish tissue—from byssus, the threads with which certain mollusks attach themselves to rocks. It is dyed with purple dyes that the ancients used, that also come from certain mollusks. The perfumes you will find in your bathroom are distilled from marine plants. Your mattress is made from seaweed. To write, you will use a pen made of whalebone. I receive everything from the sea, just as the sea will someday receive me."

"Captain, you are enamored of the sea!"

"Yes, I am. The sea is everything. It covers seven tenths of the globe. Its breath is pure and healthful. It is an immense desert where a man is never lonely, for he feels life astir on all sides. It is 'the living infinite,' as one of your poets has called it, the vast reservoir of nature. The world began with the sea, and maybe it will end with the sea. The sea does not belong to despots! Up there, on the *surface*, men can still administer unjust laws, tear one another to pieces. But thirty feet below the surface their influence is quenched. Ah, Professor, why not live—*live* in the tranquil bosom of the waters! Here only will you find true independence!"

In the midst of this enthusiasm, Captain Nemo suddenly became quite upset and paced up and down. But soon he regained his cool expression, and returned to me: "Now, Professor, if you would like to inspect the *Nautilus*, I am at your service."

VI. THE NAUTILUS

I FOLLOWED THE COMMANDER. At the back of the dining room a double door opened for us, and I entered another room of about the same size—a library!

Tall bookcases, made of black rosewood inlaid with brass, contained thousands of books, uniformly bound. They followed the shape of the room, leading at the other end to long, comfortable couches, covered with brown leather and curved to afford the greatest comfort. In the center there was an immense table, covered with pamphlets and old newspapers. Electric light, originating in four frosted globes recessed in the ceiling, flooded the room.

"This library," I said to my host, who had thrown himself onto one of the couches, "would do honor to a Continental palace! I am astounded. You have six or seven thousand books . . . ?"

"Twelve thousand, Monsieur Aronnax. These are my only ties with the land. I gave up the world the day my *Nautilus* plunged beneath the waters for the first time. From that time on, when I bought my last books, I have preferred to think that men

33

no longer write. Professor, consider these books as your own."

Thanking .him, I went up to the shelves. Works on science, ethics, literature in many languages! But not one book on political economy. That subject seemed to be strictly proscribed. Side by side were masterpieces ancient and modern, all the classics of history, poetry, and especially those of science. Books on mechanics, ballistics, meteorology and geology were almost as numerous as books on natural history, which I could see was the captain's favorite subject. In a good spot, I could see my own two volumes. Among the works of Joseph Bertrand, his *Les Fondateurs de l'Astronomie* gave me an important clue. Since I knew it had appeared in 1865, I could infer that the *Nautilus* had not been launched any earlier than that.

"Thank you for putting these treasures at my disposal, Captain," I said. "I shall surely study them with profit."

"This library, Professor, is also a smoking room. Try this cigar."

"Then you have not broken all ties with Havana?"

"It does not come from Havana, but you will like it."

I lighted it at a little brazier on a bronze stand, and drew the first whiffs with the delight of the smoker who hasn't had a puff for days. "Excellent! But it's not tobacco."

"Right. It is made from a seaweed rich in nicotine, with which the sea supplies us. Now, do you miss your London cigars?"

"Not a bit."

"Then smoke these at your pleasure."

The captain opened another door and we passed into an immense salon about thirty feet long. A high luminous ceiling, decorated with light arabesques, shed a soft light over all the marvels displayed in this . . . museum! Yes, it was a museum, in which an intelligent and prodigal hand had collected treasures of nature and of art. About thirty first-rate paintings ornamented the walls. I saw works of great value, many of which I had at one time or another admired in the special collections and exhibitions of Europe—a Madonna by Raphael, a Virgin by Leonardo, a nymph by Corregio, a woman by Titian, a monk by Velázquez, a village fair by Rubens. Among the modern works were pictures signed by Delacroix and Ingres. Admirable statues in marble and bronze stood on pedestals in the corners of the room.

"Sir," I said, "without seeking to know who you are, I am certain I know what you are—an artist."

"Only an amateur, Professor. I used to love to collect beautiful works created by the hand of man, and I have been able to bring together a few objects of great value. These are my last souvenirs of the world that is dead to me. In my eyes, the modern artists are already old—two or three thousand years old. I confuse them in my mind. The masters belong to all time."

"And these composers?" I pointed to music by Weber, Rossini, Mozart, Beethoven, Haydn, Gounod, and others scattered over an organ standing against one wall of the salon.

"These musicians are the contemporaries of Orpheus. In the memory of the dead, all chronological differences are blurred, and I am dead, Professor; as much dead as those of your friends sleeping six feet under the sod."

Captain Nemo seemed lost in reverie. I did not disturb him, but continued to study the curiosities in this splendid room.

Next to art works, natural rarities—plants, shells, other ocean products—predominated. In the center of the room, an illuminated jet of water fell back into a large fountain bowl made from the shell of a single clam. Its scalloped rim, I estimated, was at least twenty feet in circumference! And around this fountain, in elegant glass cases, I found the most precious specimens of the sea ever seen by a naturalist, and all classified and labeled! Imagine my delight! It was a collection from all parts of the world, of inestimable value, and it contained many rare specimens of shells; superb varieties of corals; and a complete collection of echinoderms. A nervous conchologist would have fainted before the cases in which the mollusks were classified. In separate cases there were also spread out a variety of pearls of the greatest beauty, which reflected the light in little sparks of fire; some were larger than a pigeon egg, and were worth more than the one owned by the Imam of Muscat, which I had believed to be unrivaled. Captain Nemo must have spent millions. I was wondering what resources he could have drawn on, so to satisfy his fancy for collecting, when I was interrupted.

"My shells must be interesting to a naturalist. But for me they have a far greater charm, because I have collected them all with my own hands, and there is not a sea I have not explored."

"I can understand your delight, Captain. No museum in Europe possesses such a collection! Still, if I exhaust my admiration on this, I shall have none left for the vessel that carries it. I do not wish to pry into your secrets, but I confess that the *Nautilus* excites my curiosity to the highest degree. For example, I see on the walls of this room some instruments entirely unfamiliar to me."

"There are identical instruments in my own room, Professor, where I shall be pleased to explain their use to you. But first come and see the cabin that I have set aside for you."

I followed Captain Nemo into a passageway. He led me toward the bow, and there I found an elegant room, with a bed, a dressing table and other furniture. I could only thank my host. "Your room adjoins mine," he said, opening another door, "and mine opens into the salon."

I entered his room, which had a severe, almost monastic air. It contained a small iron bedstead, a worktable and some chests. Captain Nemo pointed to a chair, in which I seated myself.

"Professor," he began, "there on the wall are the instruments I need to navigate the *Nautilus*. Wherever I am, I can tell my location and direction. I'm sure you recognize some of the instruments: the thermometer, which gives me the temperature inside the boat; the barometer, which helps me anticipate changes in the weather; the compass, which guides my course; the sextant, with which I can shoot the altitude of the sun and so determine my latitude; chronometers, with which I can reckon my longitude; and telescopes, with which I survey the horizon when I am upon the surface."

"So far," I said, "I recognize all the usual navigating equipment. But these other devices—this dial with the moving needle, isn't this a manometer, a pressure gauge?"

"Yes. It shows me the water pressure on our hull, and thus gives our depth."

"And these other instruments?"

"At this point I must give you some theoretical background." He paused briefly. "There is one powerful agent, the soul of our mechanical apparatus, that meets our every need. It is electricity."

"Electricity," I exclaimed, mildly surprised. "But Captain, what materials do you employ to produce this electricity? For example, do you not use zinc? And how can you replenish your supply of zinc without going into port?"

"I do not use zinc. I take my electricity from the water itself! Remember that seawater is ninety-six and a half percent water and about two and two-thirds percent sodium chloride. Mixed with mercury, the sodium extracted from the seawater forms an amalgam which can take the place of zinc in Bunsen batteries. The mercury is never consumed! Only the sodium is used up, and I can get all that I need from the sea. The electromotive force of sodium batteries, incidentally, is twice that of zinc batteries."

"Yes, the sea contains sodium," I wondered aloud. "But you still have to extract it from the sea."

"Quite. To accomplish this I heat it with coal—coal that I get from submarine mines. Remember, I owe everything to the ocean. It produces the electricity that gives life to the *Nautilus*."

"But not the air you breathe?"

"Oh, I could manufacture air if I had to, but why should I, when I can surface at will? But if electricity doesn't furnish the air, at least it works our pumps. These pumps store air under pressure in big tanks. The air in the tanks enables me to stay under as long as I have to."

"I admire what you've done, Captain. You have discovered something that someday other men will realize—the true dynamic power of electricity. It is better than wind, water, and steam."

He agreed, and showed me then still another application of electricity—a clock, run by electric current, and divided into twenty-four hours, like an Italian timepiece. "Now," he suggested after that, "let us go inspect the after part of the *Nautilus*."

So, then, I already knew the arrangement of the forward part of the boat, going from midship to the bow: a dining room about five yards long, separated by a watertight bulkhead from the library, also about five yards long; a large salon or museum, ten yards long, separated by another partition from the captain's cabin, five yards long; then my cabin, two and a half yards long; and lastly, a reservoir of air, extending about seven and a half yards to the bow. Total length, about thirty-five yards. The watertight bulkheads had doors that shut hermetically with India-rubber seals. This guaranteed the safety of the *Nautilus* in case of a leak in any one section.

Walking down the gangway, we came to the center of the boat, where there was a sort of deep well between two bulkheads. An iron ladder led upward. I asked the captain what the ladder was for.

"It leads to the dinghy that we use for fishing and sight-seeing."

"But when you want to embark, you have to surface?"

"Not at all. The boat is decked, watertight, and held down with bolts in a special cavity on the upper hull of the *Nautilus*. This ladder leads to a hatch in the hull of the *Nautilus* that corresponds to a similar hatch in the side of the dinghy. Through that double opening I enter the dinghy. The crew shuts the opening in the *Nautilus*, I shut the other one. When I undo the bolts, the dinghy shoots to the surface. Then I open the deck hatch, hoist my sail or take out my oars, and I'm off!"

After passing the staircase that led to the platform on deck, I saw a cabin about two yards long, in which Conseil and Ned were devouring their food with gusto. Then a door led to a galley about three yards long, located between two large storerooms. Electricity did all the cooking; it also heated a distilling apparatus, which produced drinking water. An adjoining bathroom was supplied with hot and cold running water! Next came the crew's quarters, about five yards long. But the door was closed, so I could not study the layout, which might have given me some idea of the size of the crew.

A door in another bulkhead was opened and I found myself in the compartment where Captain Nemo—certainly an engineer of the first order—had installed his machinery. This engine room was at least twenty yards long. It was divided into two sections, the first of which contained the equipment for generating electricity, the second, the machinery for turning the propeller. "The propeller, with a diameter of nineteen feet and a pitch of twenty-three feet, can make a hundred and twenty revolutions per second," explained the captain. "A speed of fifty knots."

"Well, having seen the *Nautilus* maneuver around the *Abraham Lincoln*, I have firsthand evidence of its swiftness. But that is not enough. You have to see where you're going. You must be able to steer to the right, left, up, down. Captain, am I being indiscreet in these inquiries?"

He hesitated. "Well, I suppose not. After all, you will never leave the *Nautilus*."

WE RETURNED TO THE SALON, where we relaxed on a divan, smoking. The captain spread out a plan of the *Nautilus*. He elaborated: "The boat you are in, Professor, is shaped much like your cigar. The length, stem to stern, is two hundred and thirty feet, and the greatest breadth of beam twenty-six feet. When entirely immersed, it displaces 1500 cubic meters—or weighs 1500 metric tons.

"When I designed it, I intended that, when floating on the surface, only one tenth would stand out of the water. Consequently, it ought to displace under these conditions nine tenths of its volume, or about 1350 cubic meters, and of course weigh that number of tons. In fact, the *Nautilus* (including her two steel hulls, one inside the other, joined by T-shaped irons for strength) weighs 1356.58 tons, or just about the desired figure. Right?"

"Right."

"So," Captain Nemo continued, "when she is afloat she is one tenth out of water. But I have built reservoirs in the lower part of her with a capacity equal to that tenth, actually able to hold 150.72 tons. When I fill them with water, the boat, now displacing 1507.2 tons, sinks just beneath the surface."

"I see that you can sink just beneath the surface, Captain. But plunging deeper, doesn't your submarine encounter a pressure, and therefore an upward thrust, of one atmosphere for every thirty-two feet of water? So, unless you fill the *Nautilus* entirely,

I don't quite see how you can force it down to any great depths."

"Professor, there is very little labor spent in reaching the bottom, for all bodies tend to sink. When I wanted to find out the necessary increase in weight required to sink the *Nautilus*, I had only to calculate the reduction in volume that seawater acquires according to depth. According to recent calculations, this reduction is only .0000436 per atmosphere, or per every thirty-two feet of depth. In order to sink thirty-two hundred feet, I must reckon the reduction in volume under a pressure of one hundred atmospheres. In this case, the reduction would be .00436. Accordingly, I would have to increase our load from 1507.2 to 1513.77 tons. The increase would be only 6.57 tons. In fact, I have supplementary tanks that can hold one hundred tons, so I can sink to quite a depth! And when I want to rise toward the surface, I pump water out."

"Accepting your calculations, Captain, I still don't see how the *Nautilus* is maneuvered."

"To steer this boat to starboard or to port, I use an ordinary rudder fixed on the stern. But I can also make the *Nautilus* go up or down by means of two movable fins fastened to the sides. They are worked by levers. If the fins are kept parallel with the boat, it moves horizontally. If they are inclined, the *Nautilus* either sinks diagonally or rises diagonally, according to their angle."

"Bravo!" I cried. "But how can the steersman follow the course underwater?"

"The helmsman is stationed in a cage, raised above the hull, and equipped with glass windows. Glass, as you perhaps know, may be shattered by a sharp blow, but it can resist tremendous pressure. During experiments with fishing by electric light in the North Sea in 1864, we saw plates less than a third of an inch thick resist a pressure of sixteen atmospheres! The glass I use is nine inches thick."

"But how can the steersman see in the dark at such depths?"

"Behind his cage I have placed a powerful electric searchlight which can light up the sea for a mile ahead."

"Ah, that accounts for the phosphorescence that was so puzzling to us. But now, how about the collision with the *Scotia?* Was that an accident?"

"Quite accidental, Professor. I was sailing only one fathom below the surface when the shock came. It had no serious effect."

"How about your collision with the *Abraham Lincoln?*"

"I'm sorry for what happened to one of the best ships in the American Navy. But she attacked me, and I had to defend myself. I contented myself, however, with simply putting the frigate out of action. She will have no trouble getting repaired."

"Your *Nautilus*, Commander, is an extraordinary ship."

"I love it, Professor, as though it were part of myself. If danger threatens a conventional vessel, your first sensation is that an abyss has opened under you! But on the *Nautilus* there are no defects to worry about, for the double shell is as firm as iron; no sails to be carried away; no boilers to burst; no fire to fear, for the vessel is not made of wood; no tempests to face, for when we dive, we reach absolute tranquillity. Here is the perfect ship! And if it is true that the engineer has more confidence in the boat than the builder has, and the builder more than the captain himself has, then you understand with what abandonment I trust my *Nautilus!* For I am captain, builder, *and* engineer!"

"Then you are an engineer by profession?"

"Oh yes, I studied in London, Paris, and New York."

"But how could you construct this boat in secret?"

"Each section was fabricated in a different part of the world. The keel was forged at Le Creusot in France; the iron plates for the hull at Laird's in Liverpool; the propeller at Scott's in Glasgow; the engines were made by Krupp in Prussia, the spur in Motala's workshop in Sweden, the precision instruments in Hart Brothers of New York, and so on. Each of these firms had my order under a different name. Then I set up my workshops on a desert island. There my workmen—these brave men that I have trained and educated—and I put together the parts. When the work was finished, we burned all evidence of our work on the island."

"This ship must have cost a great deal."

"Counting the furnishings and the collections she contains, she is worth a million dollars. But, of course, I am infinitely rich. I could, without missing it, pay off the national debt of France."

I gaped at this bizarre person as he spoke these words. Was he playing on my credulity? The future would tell.

VII. A HUNT ON THE OCEAN FLOOR

THE EARTH'S SURFACE comprises about two hundred million square miles, and it is estimated that about one hundred and forty million are underwater. In other words, water covers about ninety billion acres of our globe! During the aqueous period, ocean prevailed everywhere. By degrees, in the Silurian period, the tops of mountains began to appear, islands emerged, disappeared, reappeared, settled, and formed continents, till at length the earth became geographically arranged as we know it today. The shape of the continents divides our waters into five major oceans: the Arctic, the Antarctic, the Indian, the Atlantic and the Pacific.

The Pacific is the most tranquil of the oceans. Its currents are slow and broad, it has medium tides and abundant rain. This was the first ocean I was destined to travel under these strange auspices.

"Professor," Captain Nemo said, "it is near noon. Let us take our bearings and fix the starting point of our voyage." He pressed an electric bell three times. The pumps began to expel water from the tanks. The needle of the manometer was moving, marking the decreasing pressure on the hull. Then it stopped. "We are at the surface," he said.

I went to the central staircase, clambered up through an open hatch, and found myself topside on a railed platform three feet above water. Near the middle of the platform the dinghy, half buried in the hull of the *Nautilus*, formed a slight bulge. Fore and aft rose two cages of medium height, partly enclosed in thick, lenticular panes of glass. One was for the steersman, the other held the brilliant lantern that lighted his course. Railings and cages, I learned, could all be retracted when necessary into the hull. The bow and stern of the *Nautilus* would then form that spindle shape which had caused it to be compared to a cigar. I noticed that the iron plates on the hull, slightly overlapping each other, resembled the shell which covers the bodies of our large terrestrial reptiles. This explained why, in spite of all the intense scrutiny through telescopes, this boat had been taken for a marine animal.

The sea was beautiful, the sky pure. The long vessel could scarcely feel the broad undulations of the Pacific. A light breeze from the east rippled the waters. There was nothing in sight.

Sextant in hand, Captain Nemo was shooting the altitude of the sun in order to determine his latitude. He waited for a few moments, until in his instrument he saw its disk touch the horizon. His instrument would not have been more stable in a hand of marble. "Twelve o'clock," he said. "If you will . . ."

I cast a last look over the sea, and descended to the salon. There the captain, working with his tables and chronometer, announced: "Professor, we are at longitude 137° 15′ west."

"From which meridian?" I asked excitedly, hoping that his answer might give me a clue to his nationality!

"I have chronometers set to the meridians of Greenwich, Washington and Paris. But in your honor I am using the one for Paris."

I bowed. I had learned nothing.

"Longitude 137° 15′ west of the Paris meridian, and latitude 30° 7′ north—about three hundred miles off Japan. It is midday, November eighth, and we begin our voyage under the sea!"

"May God be with us!" I answered.

"And now I leave you to your studies. Our course is east-northeast, our depth is twenty-six fathoms. The salon is at your disposal."

He bowed and left. My eyes fell on the vast planisphere spread out on the table. Our bearings were marked on the planisphere. I placed my finger on the spot where our latitude and longitude crossed.

Now the sea, like the continents, has its large rivers. They are special currents, different from the sea around them in both temperature and color. Science has determined the directions of five. The most remarkable is known by the name of the Gulf Stream. But at the very point where my finger rested on the planisphere another of these currents was rolling: the Kuroshio, or the Black Current. This current leaves the Gulf of Bengal, where it is warmed by the rays of the tropical sun. It crosses the Strait of Malacca, follows the Asian coast and swerves into the North Pacific to the Aleutian Islands, edging the waves of the ocean with the indigo of its warm water. The *Nautilus* would now travel through it.

As I followed it with my eye, Ned and Conseil came into the salon. They seemed petrified at the wonders on display.

"Where are we?" Ned exclaimed. "In the museum at Quebec?"

"My friend," I said, "you are not in Canada, but on board the *Nautilus* fifty yards below the surface."

"Professor," he asked, "have you found out how many men there are on board?"

"I don't know, Master Land. For the time being it is better to give up any idea of seizing the *Nautilus* or escaping from it. This ship is a masterpiece of modern technology, and many people would accept our circumstances just to be able to see such marvels. So let's be calm and try to appreciate what we see."

"See! We can see nothing in this iron prison!" As Ned spoke we were suddenly plunged into utter darkness. We remained still, hearing a sliding noise, as though panels were working. "It is the end of the end!" Ned said.

Suddenly, through two oblong openings, light broke into each side of the salon. Through crystal plates, the sea, lighted by an electric gleam, was visible for a mile around us. What a spectacle! Who could describe the effects of the light through those transparent sheets of water, the softness of the successive gradations from the lower to the upper strata? The clearness of the sea is far greater than that of springwater. Mineral and organic substances that it holds in suspension heighten its transparency. But the brilliance originated in our own searchlight. It was no longer luminous water, but liquid light, and the darkness inside the salon showed to advantage the brightness outside. "You wanted to see, Ned," I said.

"Curious!" the Canadian muttered, his ill temper gone. "A man would come farther than this to see such a sight!"

"So." I was thinking about the captain. "Now I can understand him. He has made a world apart for himself, a world in which he can treasure such wonders."

"But the fish!" Ned suddenly said. "Where the devil are the fish?"

"What do you care?" Conseil teased. "You couldn't identify them anyhow."

"Me? I'm—I'm a fisherman!" Ned reminded him.

And so began a curious argument between the two friends, both of them familiar with fish, but from entirely different points of view.

Fish constitute the fourth and last class of the subdivision of vertebrates. They are defined as "vertebrates with a double circulatory system, cold-blooded, breathing through permanent gills, and destined to live in the water." There are two distinct series: bony fish, those whose spinal column is made of bony vertebrae; and cartilaginous fish, those whose spine is composed of cartilaginous vertebrae.

Maybe Ned was aware of such distinctions, but Conseil knew about them down to the last detail. "Ned," he said, "you've caught millions of fish. But I bet you can't *classify* them!"

"I sure can," the harpooner replied. "There are two distinct series: those you can eat and those you can't eat."

"But can you tell me the essential differences between bony fish and cartilaginous fish?"

"Well, the . . . now . . ."

"And how these two major classes are subdivided?"

"Well, I, er . . ."

"So listen carefully! Bony fish are subdivided into six orders, and the cartilaginous fish into three orders. Each of these orders is divided into families. The families are subdivided into genera, then subgenera, then species, and then varieties . . ."

"Well *then*"—Ned leaned against the glass—"here come your varieties!"

Marvelously, fish were now drawing near our windows. "Fish!" Conseil exclaimed. "Just like in the aquarium."

"Not exactly." I laughed. "In the aquarium, the fish are behind the glass, and here, we're the ones that are caged in. They're as free as the birds in the open air."

"Go ahead, Conseil, identify them!" Ned urged.

"I?" Conseil was astonished. "I don't do that. The professor does that."

"*Une baliste*," I said. "A triggerfish."

Yes, true, Conseil could classify fish, but he could not *recognize* them, he couldn't tell a tuna from a bonito! Ned, on the other hand, could identify each one, but couldn't classify them!

"A Chinese triggerfish," Ned specified.

"Genus, *Balistes;* family, *Sclerodermi;* order, *Plectognathi.*" Conseil completed the job.

Without a doubt, Ned and Conseil, blended as one man, would make a distinguished naturalist.

For two hours an aquatic army, apparently attracted by the brilliance of our searchlights, escorted the *Nautilus*. While they competed with each other in velocity, brightness and beauty, I identified the banded mullet, with a double black line; the Japanese scombrus, a beautiful mackerel of those waters, with blue body and silver head; the blue-gold azurors, whose name alone is their best description; serpents six feet long, with small, lively eyes and a huge mouth bristling with teeth; and many other species. We kept exclaiming as our imagination was challenged again and again. Ned named the fish, Conseil classified them. I was ecstatic, having never before been able to observe these animals in their native element.

That night, Ned and Conseil went back to their cabin and I to mine. My dinner was ready. I enjoyed turtle soup; a surmullet, the liver of which, served separately, was most delicious; and fillets of holocanthus, which seemed to me to be superior in taste even to salmon. Captain Nemo, however, did not appear.

Indeed, I passed the entire next day, November 9, without being honored by a visit from him. The panels never opened, so I resumed my study of the conchological treasures in the salon. Our course was east-northeast, our speed twelve knots, our depth ranging from twenty-five to thirty fathoms.

November 10, same desertion, same solitude. I did not see any of the crew except the steward who brought our meals. Ned and Conseil, who spent the better part of the day with me, were astonished at the captain's absence. Was he ill? Had he changed his mind about us? But we still enjoyed complete freedom of the ship and we were served great quantities of tasteful food. Our host was keeping his part of the bargain, and our situation, with its unexpected joys, gave us no right to complain.

I began that day to keep the journal of our adventures which has enabled me to recount them with scrupulous exactitude and minute detail. I wrote it on paper made from seaweed!

On November 11, at six a.m., fresh air spread through the *Nautilus*, telling me we had come to the surface to renew our oxygen supply. I mounted to the platform, where I was admiring the sunrise and inhaling the salt breeze with great delight, when I heard steps near me. It was the first officer, the man who had accompanied the captain on his first visit to us. He paid no attention to me. With his glass to his eye, he scrutinized every point of the horizon. Then he approached the hatch and pronounced a sentence in exactly these terms: *"Nautron respoc lorni virch."*

What did it mean? After uttering these words, the officer went below. I thought the *Nautilus* was about to dive, so I returned to my cabin.

Five days sped by, with no change in our situation. Every morning I mounted the platform and heard the same sentence pronounced by the same man. But Captain Nemo did not appear.

I had made up my mind that I would never see him again when, on November 16, returning to my cabin with Ned and Conseil, I found a note on my table. It was written in a bold, clear hand, suggestive of German script:

> Captain Nemo invites Professor Aronnax to a hunting party to-morrow morning in the forests of the island of Crespo. He hopes that nothing prevents the professor and the professor's friends from being present.
>
> The Commander of the *Nautilus*,
> Captain Nemo

"A hunt!" Ned exclaimed. "Does that mean he sometimes goes ashore?"

"That's what it *seems* to mean," I said. But how, I wondered to myself, can Captain Nemo hunt in a forest if he refuses as a matter of principle to go on land? "Maybe," I said aloud, "we should first find out where this island is."

Consulting the planisphere, I found, at latitude 32° 40' north and longitude 167° 50' west, a small island, visited in 1801 by Captain Crespo and marked in the old Spanish maps as *Roca de la Plata*, Silver Rock. "If Captain Nemo does occasionally go on dry ground," I said, "he certainly manages to choose desert islands."

Ned shrugged, and he and Conseil returned to their cabin.

Awaking on the morning of November 17, I felt that the *Nautilus* was perfectly still. I dressed quickly and went to the salon. Captain Nemo was waiting. He bowed, and asked if it was convenient for me to accompany him. As he made no mention of his eight-day absence, I did not mention it either, and simply answered that my companions and I were ready to go with him. We went into the dining room.

"Captain, how can you own forests on Crespo Isle when you have cut all contacts with dry land?"

"My forests are not on dry land, they are underwater."

That explained his absence. He was sick in the head. I felt sorry for him; I was sure he could see my concern in my expression.

"Professor," he said, "let us chat while we eat. I promised you a walk in the forest, but we will not find a restaurant there."

I did justice to several kinds of fish, and we drank water to which Captain Nemo added some fermented liquor, extracted from a seaweed. The captain ate in silence for a few minutes and then said, "Sir, when I proposed that we go hunting under the water, you evidently thought me mad. You should never judge any man so lightly."

"But Captain, believe me . . ."

"Professor, please listen. You know that man can live underwater if he can carry a supply of breathable air. In underwater construction jobs, the workman, clad in a diving suit, with his head in a metal helmet, can be supplied with air from above through tubes. But he has no freedom and can never wander far."

"And your means of getting free of the tubes?" I asked.

"The Rouquayrol-Denayrouze apparatus, invented by two of your countrymen. I have perfected it for my own purposes. It consists of an iron reservoir in which I can store compressed air. This tank is fastened to the back with straps, like a soldier's pack. Two tubes leave this tank and enter the copper helmet that covers the head. One tube introduces fresh air, the other leads foul air out. The breather can close one or the other with his tongue as he requires. The apparatus also recharges the compressed-air gun which you will carry on our hunt."

"Then we use an air gun?"

"Yes."

"It seems to me that in this dense fluid, shots could not go very far, nor prove fatal."

"On the contrary, with this gun every hit is fatal. However lightly the animal is touched, it falls as if struck by lightning. The bullets are little capsules invented by the Austrian chemist Leniebroek. These glass capsules are covered with steel and weighted with a pellet of lead. They are little Leyden jars, highly charged! On the slightest impact they are discharged, and the animal falls dead."

"And how can you light your way at the bottom of the ocean?"

"With the Ruhmkorff apparatus, which I fasten to my waist. It is composed of a Bunsen pile, which I work with sodium. A coil collects the electricity that is produced, and conducts it to a special lantern that contains carbonic gas. When the apparatus is turned on, this gas becomes luminous, giving out continuous white light."

The captain then led me aft. Passing Ned and Conseil's cabin, I called my companions. We came to a chamber near the engine room that was, properly speaking, both an arsenal and a dressing room. A dozen diving suits were hanging on the wall, ready for us. Ned was obviously reluctant to put one on.

"But Ned," I pointed out, "the forests of the island of Crespo are *submarine* forests."

"I see." Disappointment spread over his face as his dreams of fresh meat faded. "Well, I'll never get into one of those things unless I'm forced to."

"No one will force you, Master Land," the captain said.

"Is Conseil going to risk it?"

"Where monsieur goes, I go," Conseil answered.

At the captain's command, two sailors helped us get into these heavy, watertight suits made of seamless India rubber. The trousers ended in thick boots weighted with lead soles. The fabric of the jacket was stretched over bands of copper, protecting the chest from the crushing pressure of the water and leaving the lungs free to function. The sleeves ended in gloves. There was a vast difference between this underwater apparatus and the old cork breast-plates, waistcoats, and other contrivances used in the eighteenth century.

Captain Nemo, a Herculean companion of his, Conseil and I were soon encased! There was nothing left to do but enclose our heads in the metal helmets. Before proceeding to this operation, I asked the captain's permission to examine my gun.

A sailor handed me a simple weapon. Its large butt, hollow inside, served as a reservoir for the compressed air. In a groove in the butt there were about twenty of the electric bullets Captain Nemo had described. When one bullet was fired, automatically the next would be made ready. "Easily handled," I said. "I hope I have a chance to try it out."

Captain Nemo thrust his head into his helmet, Conseil and I followed suit. The last thing I heard was an ironical "Good hunting!" from our Canadian friend.

The jacket was topped with a copper collar, upon which the copper helmet was screwed. Three holes, protected with thick glass, allowed us to look in all directions. As soon as the helmet was in position, the Rouquayrol apparatus began to function, and I could breathe easily.

With the Ruhmkorff lamp hanging from my belt and the gun in my gloved hand, I was all set. But, imprisoned in these heavy garments, glued to the deck by my lead shoes, I found I could not take a step. I had to be pulled into a small chamber next to the wardrobe. My companions followed, towed in the same manner. A door closed on us, and we were wrapped in profound dark. I could feel coldness mounting from my feet to my chest. Evidently they were admitting water to this chamber. A door in the side of the *Nautilus* opened and I could see faint light. I stepped out onto the floor of the ocean!

Words are impotent to relate such marvels! Captain Nemo walked ahead, followed by his gigantic companion. Conseil and I walked side by side, as if a conversation were possible through our metal helmets! I no longer felt the weight of my suit or of my helmet, inside which my head rattled like an almond inside its shell.

For a good quarter of an hour we walked on fine, even sand. This dazzling, unwrinkled carpet, sown with the impalpable dust of millions of shells, reflected the rays of the sun with wondrous intensity. Will you believe me, I could see, some six fathoms down, as though I were walking in broad daylight?

The hull of the *Nautilus*, resembling a long shoal, disappeared by degrees. Soon I could discern magnificent rocks in the distance, hung with a tapestry of beautiful zoophytes. It was ten in the morning. The sun's rays struck the surface at an oblique angle, and, refracted as though passing through a prism, they shaded the edges of the flowers, rocks, plants, shells, with the seven colors of the spectrum. It was a marvelous feast for the eyes, a kaleidoscope of red, orange, yellow, green, blue, indigo, violet—the whole palette of the painter! For want of an audience with whom to communicate my reactions, I declaimed and exclaimed to myself inside the copper helmet, expending more air in vain talk than was expedient.

Clusters of pure tuft coral, prickly fungi and anemones formed a brilliant garden of flowers, with sea stars studding the sandy bottom, together with waving asterophytons like fine lace embroidered by naiads. It was a real grief to me to crush underfoot the brilliant specimens of mollusks which strewed the ground by thousands, but we had to keep moving. So we went on, while above our heads waved shoals of Portuguese men-of-war, leaving their tentacles to float in their train; and medusae, whose umbrellas of opal or rose pink, scalloped with a band of blue, sheltered us from the rays of the sun.

In a quarter of a mile the nature of the soil changed. Leaving the sand, we walked into slimy mud, composed of equal parts of siliceous and calcareous shells. We then traveled over a plain of wild and luxuriant vegetation. This sward was of close texture, rivaling the softest carpet woven by the hand of man. A light network of seaweeds grew on the surface of the ocean, and I noticed that the green plants stayed closer to the top, while the red ones were deeper down, leaving to the black and brown hydrophytes the task of forming gardens and flower beds in the lower strata.

We had been walking now for about an hour and a half. It was nearly noon: I could tell by the perpendicularity of the sun's rays, which were no longer refracted. The magical colors disappeared by degrees. We walked with a regular step, which rang upon the ground with astonishing intensity. The slightest noise was transmitted with a speed to which the ear is unaccustomed on land, for water is a better and faster conductor of sound than air.

The earth sloped downward. We were one hundred yards down, withstanding a pressure of nearly ten atmospheres! Even at this depth I could still see the sun's rays, though feebly. Their brilliance had changed to a reddish twilight. Captain Nemo stopped and waited for me to catch up. He pointed to an obscure mass looming in the shadow a short distance away. At last we had reached the edge of the forest of the island of Crespo, probably one of the most beautiful of Captain Nemo's vast domains.

It was a forest of large tree plants. The moment we entered its vast arcades, I was struck by the unique position of the branches. They all stretched straight up! Every filament, no matter how thick or thin, stood straight as an iron rod. They seemed incapable of motion, but when I pushed them to one side they immediately resumed their former position. This was the land of perpendicularity!

Soon I adjusted to this bizarre situation and to the darkness that enveloped us. The forest soil seemed covered with sharp blocks, difficult to avoid. Occasionally I took zoophytes to be hydrophytes, animals to be plants. I think anybody would have made the same

error. "Curious anomaly, bizarre element," one ingenious naturalist has said, "in which the animal kingdom flowers, and the vegetable kingdom does not!" Under such plants—some as big as trees—
were massed together real bushes of living flowers, hedges of zoophytes; and to complete the illusion, fish flies flew from branch to
branch like swarms of hummingbirds, while lepisachanthae and
monocentridae rose at our feet like flights of snipe!

In about an hour the commander signaled us to halt. We
stretched out under an arbor of alariae. In this short rest, there
was nothing lacking but the charm of conversation. Unable to
talk or listen, I could only put my big copper head next to Conseil's. His eyes glistened with delight through the glass pane. I felt
a passionate desire to sleep, a feeling that I understand comes over
all divers. Captain Nemo and his companion were already stretched
out and motionless. My eyes closed and I fell into a deep slumber.

When I woke it seemed to me the sun was sinking toward the
horizon. I was looking around lazily when an unexpected apparition brought me to my feet. A monster sea spider three feet high
was squinting at me, poised to spring. Though my diver's dress
was thick enough to protect me from the creature, I shuddered with
horror. Fortunately the others were getting up too, and Captain
Nemo's companion knocked over the hideous crustacean with the
butt of his gun. But the encounter reminded me that other and
more fearful animals might haunt these deeps, animals against
which my suit would be little protection. Indeed, as Captain Nemo
continued his bold expedition, I determined to be more alert.

The ground still declined, and it must have been three in the
afternoon when we reached a narrow gorge seventy-five fathoms
deep. At ten paces nothing was visible. I was groping my way
when suddenly I saw a bright white light. Captain Nemo had just
turned on his Ruhmkorff lamp. I turned on mine, and soon the sea,
lighted by four such lamps, was illuminated for a hundred feet
all around us.

Captain Nemo was plunging deeper into the forest. The trees
were becoming scarcer. Vegetable life was disappearing faster
than animal life. It occurred to me that our lights would probably

draw some inhabitant from its dark couch. Several times I saw Captain Nemo stop, shoulder his gun, drop it, and walk on.

At last an enormous steep granite mass rose before us, forming dark grottoes but offering no surfaces up which one could climb. It was the shore of the island of Crespo! It was the earth!

With a gesture Captain Nemo halted our trip. Here ended his domains, and he would not go beyond them.

The return began. By a different route we regained the upper strata rapidly, keeping in mind that sudden changes in pressure could bring on internal lesions, "the bends," that dread disease of divers. Very soon, light from the rays of the sun reappeared.

At a depth of thirty feet again, we were walking amid a shoal of little fishes more numerous than the birds of the air. There still had been no aquatic game worthy of a shot. Then suddenly I saw the captain shoulder his gun and follow a moving object into the shrubs. He fired, I actually heard a slight hissing, and a creature fell dead some distance away.

It was a magnificent sea otter, the only exclusively marine quadruped. It was five feet long and its skin, chestnut above and silver underneath, would have made a beautiful fur, certainly fetching four hundred dollars. Captain Nemo's Herculean companion tossed the beast over his shoulder and we continued our journey homeward.

For an hour, a plain of sand lay stretched before us. Sometimes it rose to within six feet of the surface. Then I could see our image clearly reflected, and above us there walked an identical group, like us in every way except that they walked with heads down and feet in the air. Another unusual effect that I noticed was the passage of thick clouds, which formed and vanished rapidly. I soon realized that these "clouds" were due to the varying depth of the water over a ground swell; I could see the foam breaking on the crests and spreading over the surface. I also saw the shadows of big birds that skimmed overhead.

Thus I witnessed one of the finest gunshots that ever thrilled a hunter. A bird of great wingspread hovered over us. Captain Nemo's companion fired his gun. The creature fell, and the force of its fall brought it within the hunter's grasp. It was a superb albatross.

For two hours we had followed these sandy plains when I saw a glimmer of light half a mile away. It was the searchlight of the *Nautilus*. I was thinking that within twenty minutes we should be on board when suddenly I saw Captain Nemo rushing toward me. With a strong push he flung me to the ground. His companion pushed Conseil down. I did not know what to make of this sudden attack, but I was reassured to see the captain and his Hercules also stretched out.

Raising my head a bit over a bush of algae, my blood froze. I saw two formidable sharks. Two tintoreas; terrible creatures, with huge tails and dull, glassy stares—monsters that can crush a man in their jaws! I don't know whether Conseil took the trouble to classify them. Speaking for myself, I looked at their silver bellies, their huge mouths bristling with teeth, from a very unscientific viewpoint.

Fortunately these voracious beasts do not see well. They passed by without seeing us, brushing us with their brown fins.

Later, as I shed my diving suit in the *Nautilus*, I realized that miraculously we had escaped a danger greater than meeting a tiger face-to-face in the forest.

VIII. FOUR THOUSAND LEAGUES UNDER THE PACIFIC

NEXT MORNING, after I had recovered from the hunt, I went up on the platform just as the lieutenant was uttering his daily phrase. It then occurred to me that this expression meant something like "There is nothing in sight." The ocean was deserted. The heights of Crespo had disappeared. The sea was a marvelous indigo.

And then, while I was admiring the magnificent aspect of the ocean, Captain Nemo appeared. Apparently unaware of my presence, he made a series of astronomical observations and later leaned on the cage of the lantern and gazed abstractedly out to sea. Meanwhile, a score of sailors also ascended to the platform. They were evidently of many nationalities, but they spoke very little, and then in that odd language the origin of which I could not even guess at.

They were hauling in the fishnets that had been dragging along the sea floor for many hours now. That day they brought up curious specimens from those coasts—frogfish, or anglerfish, comical as clowns; triggerfish, circled with red bands; poisonous globefish; olive-colored lampreys; trichiuri, whose electric shock equals that of the electric eel; some excellent bonitos, streaked with blue and silver; and three splendid tuna. I estimated that they were hauling in a thousand pounds of fish. This enormous catch was lowered down the hatch to the galley, some to be served fresh, the rest to be pickled.

With the fishing over and our air supply renewed, I thought we were about to dive, and started below. But unexpectedly the captain turned to me and said, "Professor, this ocean is gifted with real life! It has its tempers and its gentle moods. It rested as we did, and now it has awakened."

No "Good day," no "Hello." It was as though he were simply resuming a conversation we had begun earlier.

"Look! It wakes under the caresses of the sun. It is renewing its diurnal existence. It has a pulse, arteries, spasms. I agree with the learned Maury, who discovered that the ocean has a circulation as real as the circulation of blood in animals."

I was sure he expected no reply, and it seemed pointless to say "Oh yes," or "How right you are." He was talking to himself, with pauses between sentences.

"Yes, to keep the ocean's circulation going, the Creator has only to change its temperature or its salinity, or to multiply its animalcules. Temperature change varies the density, causing currents and countercurrents. Salts make the waters less evaporable, so winds cannot pick up too much vapor, which would flood the temperate zones. And microscopic organisms absorb marine salt, assimilate the solid elements in the water, and, by making corals, or madrepores, they build calcareous continents. This sea that people call a medium of death is a medium of life. . . . Down there, I can imagine the founding of nautical towns, clusters of submarine houses that, like the *Nautilus*, would rise every day to breathe at the surface—free towns, independent cities. But, still, who knows whether or not some . . . despot . . ."

He ended his monologue with a violent gesture. Talking directly to me as though to chase away some sorrowful thought, he asked, "Do you know the real depth of the ocean, Professor?"

"I only know, Captain, what the principal soundings have indicated. The most remarkable have been made in the South Atlantic, near the thirty-fifth parallel, and they gave thirty-six to forty-five thousand feet."

"Well, Professor, I hope we shall show you better than that. As to the mean depth of this part of the Pacific, I can tell you it is only twelve thousand feet."

Captain Nemo made for the hatch and disappeared down the ladder. After I went down into the salon, the propeller began to turn and soon the log showed we were traveling at twenty knots.

I seldom saw Captain Nemo in the days and weeks following. The lieutenant would mark the ship's course on the chart, so that I could always tell exactly the route of the *Nautilus*. Our general direction was southeast, our depth three hundred to four hundred and fifty feet. Almost every day the side panels opened, and we never tired of penetrating the mysteries of the undersea world.

On November 26, we crossed the Tropic of Cancer at longitude 172° west. On the twenty-seventh we sighted the Hawaiian Islands, where Cook had died on February 14, 1779. We crossed the equator at longitude 142° on December 1. By December 11, we had traveled a further two thousand miles.

I was reading on that day in the large salon, and Ned and Conseil were watching the luminous water through the open panels. The *Nautilus* was not moving. With tanks full, it stayed at a depth of three thousand feet, in this region of the ocean where only large fish are found. Suddenly Conseil interrupted my reading. "Would monsieur come here a moment?"

In the full electric light, an enormous black mass, motionless, was suspended in the water. I watched, hoping to ascertain the nature of this cetacean. Then a thought hit me. "A ship!" I said.

"Yes," Ned said, "a disabled ship that has sunk straight down."

He was right. We were close to a vessel whose tattered shrouds still hung from their chains—the first of many marine disasters that we were to encounter on our voyage. This ship had been wrecked only a few hours before. The hull seemed to be intact. Three stumps of masts, broken off about two feet above the deck, showed that the captain had sacrificed his masts in an effort to save the hull and the people aboard. But lying over on its side, the ship had filled, and was heeling to port. This skeleton of what it once had been was a sad sight as it hung lost under the waves. But sadder still was the sight on the decks, where some corpses, bound with ropes, still stood—four men, one of them at the helm, and one woman near the poop holding an infant in her arms. She was young. By the brilliant light of the *Nautilus* I could make out her features. The baby's arms still encircled the mother's neck. The postures of the sailors were frightful, distorted as they were by the last convulsive movements they had made in trying to free themselves from the ropes that lashed them to the ship. The helmsman, calm, with a grave face and gray hair pasted to his forehead, still clutched the wheel, and seemed even now to be guiding the broken three-master through the deep.

We were dumbfounded. Even as we watched, enormous sharks, attracted by human flesh, came toward the shipwreck with hungry eyes. Then the *Nautilus* moved around the submerged ship and I could read, on the stern: *The Florida, Sunderland.*

The terrible sight had hardly vanished before we came within view of the Tuamotu Archipelago, which extends five hundred leagues from east-southeast to west-northwest. Covering an area of three hundred and seventy square leagues, it is formed of sixty groups of coral islands, actually built out of the sea, slowly but constantly, by the daily toil of microscopic polyps. These tiny animals can extract calcium from seawater and deposit it around them as calcium carbonate, or limestone. As a colony produces new polyps, old members die and new layers are built up on the skeletons of the dead. Each polyp contributes to the communal life, yet has a life of its own. It is a sort of natural socialism.

Someday they may actually build links between their isles, and a new continent may extend from New Zealand and New Caledonia all the way to the Marquesas!

When I suggested this to Captain Nemo, he replied coolly, "Professor, we don't need new continents, we need new men."

By December 25, the *Nautilus* had sailed into the New Hebrides. We passed near the island of Aurou, which at noon looked like a mass of greenwoods surmounted by a great peak. Christmas, the family holiday, was not observed—much to Ned's resentment.

WE CONTINUED ON A southwesterly course; and early on the morning of January 1, 1868, Conseil joined me on the platform. "Will monsieur permit me to wish him a Happy New Year?"

"Thank you Conseil, and the same to you! But by a 'happy new year' do you mean a year that sees the end of our imprisonment, or a year that sees us continuing this strange voyage?"

"I suppose, with no offense to monsieur, that a happy new year would be the one in which we see all the marvels but get them over with!"

By January 2 we had made 5250 French leagues, or 11,340 miles, since the start of our trip in the Sea of Japan. Before us stretched the Coral Sea and the dangerous reefs on the northeast coast of Australia. But by January 5 we had sighted the coast of New Guinea. Then Captain Nemo informed me that he intended to get into the Indian Ocean by the Torres Strait!

The Torres Strait is nearly thirty-four leagues wide, but obstructed by numerous islands and rocks that make its navigation almost impracticable. Captain Nemo took the necessary precautions. Floating between wind and water, the *Nautilus* ran southeast to northwest at two and a half knots, her propeller slowly beating the waves like a cetacean's tail.

My companions and I went up onto the deserted platform. We sat behind the steersman's cage. I surmised that Captain Nemo was in there himself, directing our course. The sea dashed around us furiously.

"A bad sea!" said Ned. "The captain must be quite sure of his way. I can see coral rocks that would ruin our keel if it just touched them slightly."

The situation was perilous, but our boat seemed to slide like magic through these rocks until full tide at three p.m. Suddenly I was thrown to the deck. When I got up, I saw the *Nautilus* had hit one of the rocks and lay slightly to her port side, motionless! Captain Nemo and his lieutenant appeared on the platform to study the position of the boat.

The *Nautilus* was situated thus: two miles to starboard appeared Gueboroar Island, stretched from north to west like an immense arm. Toward the south and east we could see coral formations. We had run aground at high tide in one of those seas where tides are middling—a sorry matter. True, the vessel herself had not suffered, but if she could not float off, she would be done for.

These thoughts were racing through my head when Captain Nemo, always master of himself, came over to me. "An accident?" I asked.

"No, an incident."

"But an incident that may force you to dwell on land again!"

"Professor, the *Nautilus* is not done for. Our voyage is only begun. I do not want to be deprived so soon of your company."

"But Captain, the tides are not strong in the Pacific. If you cannot lighten the *Nautilus*, how can she be floated again?"

"You are right about the tides, but there is still a difference here of five feet between high and low seas. Today is January fifth. In four days the moon will be full. I shall be astonished if that obliging satellite does not raise these waters enough to render me a service!"

Captain Nemo and his lieutenant went below. The *Nautilus* remained motionless, as if the coralline polyps had already fastened it with their indestructible cement. Ned and Conseil came over to me and I told them what the captain had said.

The Canadian shrugged his shoulders. "Take my word for it, Professor, this piece of scrap iron will navigate neither on nor under the ocean again. I think, therefore, that the time has come to part company with Captain Nemo."

"Ned, I have more faith in the *Nautilus* than that. But in any

And best of all, the Abraham Lincoln *had on board Ned Land, prince of harpooners.*

The monster that had intrigued the world of science, and confused the imagination of seamen from two hemispheres, was an even more astonishing phenomenon—a man-made thing shaped like an immense steel fish.

"This library," I said to my host, who had thrown himself onto one of the couches, "would do honor to a Continental palace!"

Sextant in hand, Captain Nemo was shooting the altitude of the sun in order to determine his latitude.

Marvelously, fish were now drawing near our windows.

With tanks full, it stayed at a depth of three thousand feet, in this region of the ocean where only large fish are found.

Conseil seized his gun and aimed at a savage who was balancing his sling . . . just ten yards or so away.

But he fled, uttering cries of terror, his body contorting wildly. . . . Captain Nemo had electrified the stair rail!

event, we shall have our answer in five days. Escape would be easy if we were off the coast of England or Provence, but off the coast of New Guinea, that's a different thing! And it will be time enough to think of that if the *Nautilus* fails to right herself."

"But look! There is an island. On that island there are land animals, bearers of meat, which I would love to get my teeth into again!"

"Ned is right about that," Conseil said. "Could monsieur get permission from the captain to go on land? Just so we don't lose the knack of walking on the solid part of our planet?"

"I can ask, but I know he will say no."

But to my great surprise Captain Nemo said yes, and he said it very agreeably, without even exacting from me a promise to return to the ship! But of course I should have discouraged Ned from attempting flight across New Guinea. Better to be a prisoner on the *Nautilus* than to fall into the hands of savages!

Armed with guns and hatchets, we got off the *Nautilus* at eight o'clock next morning. The sea was quite calm. A slight breeze was blowing from the land. With Conseil and me at the oars, and Ned steering, we sped along. Ned could not restrain his joy. "Meat! We're going to eat meat!" he kept saying.

"It remains to be seen," I cautioned, "whether the island's forests really are full of game, and whether that game is the kind that hunts the hunter."

"Neatly put," Ned said. "But"—and his teeth seemed as sharp as the edge of his hatchet—"if there is no other quadruped on this island, I am perfectly willing to eat loin of tiger."

At half past eight, after happily passing the coral reef that surrounds Gueboroar, we ran gently aground on sand. We were tremendously excited to be on land again. In just a few moments we were a musket shot away from the surf! The horizon was hidden behind a beautiful curtain of forest. Enormous trees, perhaps two hundred feet tall, were tied to each other with garlands of bindweed, natural hammocks that could be rocked by a light breeze. They were mimosas, teaks and palm trees. Under the shelter of their verdant vaults grew orchids, vegetables, ferns. Ned, finding a coconut tree, beat down some of its coconuts and cracked them open. We drank the milk and ate the meat with great pleasure.

"Excellent!" sighed Ned. "I don't think your friend Captain Nemo could object to our bringing coconuts on board."

"Maybe. But I'm sure he won't eat any himself."

"So much the better for us," replied Ned.

"Just one word, Master Land," I said to the harpooner, who was about to ravage another coconut tree. "Before filling the dinghy with coconuts, maybe we should see if the island produces any other fruits or vegetables. But let's be very careful. The place seems uninhabited, but it might still contain people less interested in *wild* life than we are!"

"Ho, ho, ho!" Ned moved his jaws significantly. "I begin to understand the charms of cannibalism."

"Let's go," said Conseil. "We must at least shoot some game to satisfy this meat eater, or else, one of these mornings, monsieur will find only pieces of servant left to serve him!"

For two hours we walked under the somber arches of the forest, exploring in all directions and gathering bananas, mangoes and pineapples. Then we had the good luck to find a breadfruit tree. Ned had eaten this fruit on his many voyages, and he knew how to cook it. Armed with a magnifying glass, he lighted a fire of dead wood. While it crackled joyously, Conseil and I picked a dozen of the ripest fruits on the tree, those that were yellow and gelatinous. Ned cut them into thick slices and placed them over his fire. In a few minutes the slices were toasted. The inside looked like a white pastry, with a soft crumb. It tasted something like an artichoke, and I ate it with great gusto.

"Now," said Ned, "what about looking for the roast?"

To humor the Canadian, Conseil and I followed him toward the west until he gained a plateau that was bordered by a forest alive with birds. In the thick foliage were chattering parrots, parakeets of many colors, solemn cockatoos that seemed to be meditating philosophy, and brilliant red lories; all in all, a variety of winged things, charming to behold but not good to eat!

Next, passing through a moderately thick coppice, we could see those magnificent birds that are peculiar to these lands! The arrangement of their long feathers makes it necessary for them to fly against the wind. I was charmed by their undulating flight, their graceful curves in the air, the nuances of their colors. "Birds of paradise!" I exclaimed.

The Malays have ways of taking these birds that we could not employ. They put snares at the tops of the high trees where the birds perch, and they even poison the streams that the birds drink from. All we could do was to fire vainly at them in the air.

By two p.m. we had crossed the foothills of the mountains that form the center of the island, and still we had killed nothing. Turning back toward the coast, we reached a forest of sago trees. Harmless snakes glided away from under our feet. The birds of paradise fled at our approach, and I despaired of getting near one, when suddenly Conseil, walking ahead of us, bent down, uttered a cry of triumph, and came back to me with a magnificent specimen.

"Bravo, Conseil! What a feat to capture one of those birds alive!"

"If monsieur will examine the bird, he will see I do not deserve such praise. The bird is drunk!"

"Drunk?"

"Drunk from the nutmegs it devoured under the nutmeg tree, where I found it! See, Ned, the monstrous effects of intemperance!"

I examined the bird and found that Conseil was right. The bird was helpless. It was a "great emerald bird," the most rare and beautiful of all the species. It was a foot long, with a pale yellow head, yellow beak, nut-colored wings with purple tips, emerald-colored throat and chestnut breast and belly. The natives have poetically called this marvelous creature "the bird of the sun."

"I'll be happy to give this bird to the Jardin des Plantes—they don't have a live specimen."

"You mean they're rare?" Ned asked.

"So rare, Ned, that natives sell fake ones. During the monsoon season, these birds of paradise lose their feathers. Some natives pick them up, attach them to parakeets, varnish their forgeries, and sell them to collectors."

My fondest wish fulfilled, I thought now of Ned's. Happily,

about three o'clock he brought down with his air gun a magnificent hog, the kind the natives call *bari-outang*. Proudly, he skinned and cleaned it, taking half a dozen chops for our evening meal. Next, beating the bushes, Ned and Conseil roused a herd of kangaroo hares that bounded away on their elastic paws. But they could not outspeed our bullets.

"What excellent game!" Ned was shouting. "What a supply for the *Nautilus!* Two! Three! Five down! *We* will eat that meat. The idiots in the crew won't get a bit of it!"

I think if Ned had not talked so much he might have killed every one of them. But he had to be content with a mere dozen of these small marsupials that live in the hollows of trees.

We regained the shore and our dinghy by six p.m. Some distance from the beach we could see the *Nautilus*, like a long rock. Without a moment's delay, Ned got down to making dinner. As he grilled the bari-outang over his coals, a delicious odor filled the air. Our excellent menu also comprised sago paté, breadfruit slices, mangoes, pineapples and coconut milk.

"Suppose we don't go back to the *Nautilus* tonight?" Conseil said.

"Suppose we never go back?" said Ned.

At that moment a stone fell at our feet, putting an end to our supposing. My hand stopped halfway to my mouth. Without rising we stared into the forest.

"A stone doesn't fall out of the sky," observed Conseil, "or it would be called a meteorite."

A second stone, well aimed, knocked a pineapple out of his hand. We reached for our rifles.

"Apes?" Ned hypothesized.

"Savages," Conseil said.

"To the boat!" I raced toward the water.

Indeed it was necessary to beat a quick retreat. About twenty natives, brandishing bows and slings, had emerged from a coppice a hundred paces to our right. Stones and arrows rained about us!

Unwilling to abandon his provisions, Ned carried the remains of his hog over one shoulder and his kangaroo hares over the other, and still made good time. In two minutes we reached the shore. To load the boat and to push out to sea was the work of just another minute. And by the time we were two cable lengths from the beach there were a hundred howling savages out in the water up to their waists. I watched to see whether this spectacle would induce any-one on board the *Nautilus* to come out on the platform. But no. The enormous machine seemed to be absolutely deserted.

In twenty minutes we were on board. I could hear music coming from the salon. Captain Nemo was there, bent over his organ.

"Captain!" Deep in a musical ecstasy, he did not hear me. "Captain!" I touched his hand.

He shuddered and turned around. "Ah, it's you, Professor. How was the hunting? Any good botanical specimens?"

"Oh, yes, Captain. But unfortunately we attracted a troop of bipeds! Their proximity disturbs me."

"What bipeds?"

"Savages!"

"Savages," he repeated ironically. "So, Professor, you set foot on a strange land and you are astonished to find savages? What land doesn't have its own kind of savage, Professor?"

"But, Captain . . . there are at least a hundred."

"Monsieur Aronnax"—he placed his fingers on the stops of his organ—"when all the Papuan natives assemble on this shore, the *Nautilus* still will have nothing to fear."

As his fingers ran over the keys, he was plunged once more into a reverie. Not wishing to disturb him again, I went up on the platform. Night had already fallen. In this low latitude, the sun sets suddenly and with no twilight. I could see the island only indis-tinctly. But numerous fires along the beach showed clearly that the natives had no intention of leaving it. By now, however, I had no fear of the Papuans, for our captain's calm was catching.

That night and the next day slipped by with no misadventures. Perhaps the islanders were frightened at the thought of a monster aground in the bay. However, when I went out on the platform at six on the morning of January 8 I noticed that there were now as many as five or six hundred natives on the beach. Some of them, taking advantage of the low tide, had come out on the coral less than two cable lengths from the *Nautilus*.

They were true Papuans, with athletic figures, large high foreheads and white teeth. Most of them were naked. Their woolly, red-tinged hair contrasted clearly with their shiny black bodies. Nearly all the men were armed with bows, arrows, slings, shields, and carried on their shoulders nets containing the round stones that they used for sling shot.

First, a chief came close to the *Nautilus* and studied it carefully. Perhaps he was a *mado* of high rank, for he was draped in a mat of banana leaves notched around the edges and brightly painted. He was followed by some companions and soon, during the low tide, many natives were wandering about near the *Nautilus*, but causing no trouble. I heard them often saying "*Assai*," and from their gestures I inferred that they were inviting me to come on land, an invitation I declined.

About eleven in the morning, the coral began to disappear under the rising tide, and the natives returned to the shore. I could see their numbers increasing on the beach. Perhaps others were coming from neighboring islands. But I had not yet seen a single native canoe. Wondering how to pass the time, I decided I would drag these beautiful clear waters for shells, zoophytes and plants. After all, it was the last day we would be spending in these parts, if the *Nautilus* righted herself when the captain expected!

Conseil brought me a little light drag, like those used for oysters. And to work! For two hours we fished from the *Nautilus'* platform without finding anything unusual. Then, just when I least expected it, I put my hand on a rarity, I might say a natural deformity. Conseil heard me utter a conchological cry—that is, the most piercing cry the human throat can utter!

"What is the matter? Has monsieur been bitten?"

"No, my boy, but I would willingly give a finger for this shell," I said, holding up my great find.

"That is simply an olive porphyry."

"Yes, of course, Conseil. But instead of being rolled from right to left, this olive turns from left to right!"

"A left-handed shell! Ah, monsieur, I can hardly believe it," he said, taking the precious shell with a trembling hand. Shells are right-handed, with rare exceptions. And when by chance their whorl is left, connoisseurs are willing to pay their weight in gold.

We were contemplating our treasure, and I was thinking how happy they would be at the museum to have it, when a stone struck and broke the precious object in Conseil's hand. I cried out in despair. Conseil seized his gun and aimed at a savage who was balancing his sling from a canoe, just ten yards or so away. I tried to stop Conseil, but too late—his shot shattered a bracelet of amulets around the man's arm.

"Conseil! Conseil!" I cried. "A shell is not worth a man's life."

"The scoundrel," Conseil said. "I would rather he had broken my shoulder than that shell!"

He was sincere, but I did not share his opinion. However, it was obvious that the situation had changed and we had not been alert to it. Twenty or so canoes now appeared and surrounded the *Nautilus*. Made of hollowed-out tree trunks, these canoes were long, narrow and fast; they were balanced by means of long bamboo pontoons floated on the water.

As the canoes neared the *Nautilus*, a shower of arrows fell around us. I knew that our weapons, which were noiseless, could have little effect on the native paddlers, who could be impressed only with loud blustering things. I raced down to the salon, but no one was there. I knocked at the captain's door.

"Come in."

"I know I am disturbing you."

The captain looked up from papers covered with mathematical symbols. "Yes, Professor," the captain replied. "But I assume you have good reasons?"

"Very serious reasons. The natives have surrounded us. In a moment we shall be attacked by hundreds of warriors in canoes!"

"Then we must close the hatches."

"Yes, and I came to say that—"

"Nothing could be simpler." He pressed a button, transmitting a signal to his crew. "That is all there is to it. The dinghy is in its proper place. The hatches are closed. You do not think, I hope, that these gentlemen could stave in a hull on which your cannonballs had no effect?"

"No, Captain, but there is still one danger."

"What is that?"

"Tomorrow we must open the hatches to renew our air supply. What then will keep the Papuans from entering the *Nautilus?*"

"So you think they will board us."

"Why not?"

"Let them come. I see no reason for stopping them. I do not want my visit to Gueboroar Island to cost the life of a single one of these poor wretches. Besides, tomorrow, at exactly two forty p.m., the *Nautilus* shall float and leave the Torres Strait."

Pronouncing these words, he bowed. Having been dismissed, I returned to my cabin.

That night I slept poorly, thanks to the noise of the savages, who stamped about on the platform, uttering deafening cries. I got up at six a.m. The hatches had not been opened. And so our air supply had not been renewed. But now Captain Nemo resorted to his emergency tanks, which discharged fresh oxygen into the stale atmosphere on board.

I worked for hours, first in my cabin and then in the salon, without once seeing the captain. Suddenly I noticed that it was half past two! In ten minutes it would be high tide! If Captain Nemo had not miscalculated, the *Nautilus* would soon be afloat! If he had erred . . .

But now I could feel some movement. I could hear the keel grating against the reef. At two thirty-five Captain Nemo appeared in the salon. "We're ready to go," he said.

"Ah!" was all I could say.

"I've given the order to open the hatches."

"But the Papuans! Won't they come down them?"

"No. Come along and watch."

I walked toward the central staircase. Conseil and Ned were watching the sailors who were opening the hatches. From outside came cries of fierce rage.

As soon as the port hatch was opened, twenty warlike faces looked down on us. Then one native put his hand on the stair rail and . . . Had he been struck from behind? I could not tell. But he fled, uttering cries of terror, his body contorting wildly. Ten of his companions tried the descent. Ten fled in the same way.

Conseil was in ecstasy. But Ned, carried away by his love of violence, rushed up to the staircase. He seized the stair rail with both hands, and he too was violently overthrown! "I've been hit by lightning!" he exclaimed.

That explained everything! Captain Nemo had electrified the stair rail! And whoever touched it felt a powerful shock. Paralyzed with terror, the Papuans had beat a retreat. Half laughing, we consoled and massaged poor Ned Land, who cursed away like one possessed.

And now the *Nautilus*, gently lifted by the last wave of the tide, left her coral bed at exactly two forty p.m. With her propeller beating the waters slowly and majestically, she passed safe and sound through the perilous Strait of Torres.

IX. THE CORAL KINGDOM

THE *Nautilus* HEADED quickly southwest toward the Indian Ocean. Skirting the sands of Cartier Island and Scott Reef, we lost sight of land altogether on January 14. The *Nautilus* slowed down, and sometimes swam in the bosom of the waters, sometimes on the surface.

During this phase of our voyage, Captain Nemo made some interesting observations on the varying temperature of the sea at different depths and latitudes. Usually, such observations are made by means of instruments that must be lowered from the surface. Results so obtained cannot be correctly evaluated. Captain Nemo was of course able to go down himself to measure the temperature, and his thermometers, read on the spot, gave him the most accurate data ever obtained. His definite conclusion was that the sea maintains, at a depth of five hundred fathoms, an average temperature of four and a half degrees Centigrade or forty degrees Fahrenheit, regardless of latitude.

Then we conducted experiments on the salinity of water at different depths, its electrical nature, coloration and transparency; and throughout these investigations Nemo displayed an ingenuity equaled only by his graciousness.

On January 16, the ship seemed becalmed just a few yards beneath the surface. Her engines and generators were idle, leaving her to drift at the mercy of the currents. I supposed that the crew were making repairs. My companions and I then witnessed a curious spectacle. The panels of the salon were open, and since the searchlight was not in use a dim obscurity reigned in the midst of the water. Under these conditions the largest fish appeared to me as scarcely defined shadows. Then suddenly the *Nautilus* was surrounded by strong light. I thought at first that the searchlight had been turned on, but I was wrong.

The *Nautilus* was floating through a phosphorescent stratum that, in this obscurity, became quite dazzling. It was produced by myriads of luminous animalcules, whose brilliance was intensified as they glided over the metal hull of the submarine. And then, in the midst of all this illumination, there seemed to be flashes of lightning, as though masses of metal had been brought to a white heat, so that by sheer force of contrast some areas of the light actually cast a shadow in the overall brightness! No, this was not the calm irradiation of our ordinary lighting. Here were vitality and vigor. Here was *living* light!

For this was an infinite agglomeration of tiny noctilucae, globules of diaphanous jelly provided with threadlike tentacles. As many as twenty-five thousand have been counted in one ounce of water.

For hours the *Nautilus* floated in these brilliant waves. We marveled as we watched the marine monsters disporting themselves like salamanders. In the midst of this fire that does not burn, I saw the swift, elegant porpoise—the tireless clown of the ocean—and some swordfish ten feet long whose formidable swords would now and then strike the glass panels. Then came the smaller fish, the triggerfish, the leaping mackerel, wolffish and scores of others which streaked the luminous medium!

And so we spent our time, charmed always by new wonders. Conseil arranged and classed his zoophytes, his mollusks, his fishes. Ned tried to vary the ship's menu. The hours sped by, and I took no account of them. Like snails, we were attached to our shell, and I declare, it is easy to lead a snail's life. We thought no longer of the life we had led on land—until January 18.

The *Nautilus* was in longitude 105° latitude 15° south. The weather was ominous, the sea rough and rolling. There was a strong east wind, and the barometer had been dropping. I went up on the platform just as the lieutenant was taking our position. I waited, as usual, to hear his daily sentence. But on this day he uttered a different sentence.

Almost immediately, Captain Nemo came up. He and his glass were absolutely motionless as he studied a point on the horizon indicated by his lieutenant. Then he talked with his lieutenant, who seemed to be answering with passionately strong assurances. For myself, I could see nothing at all in the direction indicated. Sky and water met in a clear line.

Now Captain Nemo walked from one end of the platform to the other without looking at me. His step was firm but not so regular as usual. Sometimes he stopped, crossed his arms, and stared at the sea. What could he be looking for in that great expanse? The *Nautilus* was hundreds of miles from the nearest shore.

Again the lieutenant was pointing out something on the horizon. He seemed greatly agitated. Puzzled, I went down to the salon and took out an excellent telescope that I often used myself. I climbed up again and, leaning on the cage of the searchlight, started to scan the horizon. But as soon as I had put the glass to my eye it was snatched from my hands.

I turned around to face Captain Nemo. His features were transfigured. His eyes flashed. His teeth were set. His body was stiff, his fists clenched. My glass rolled on the platform. Had I provoked this furious agitation? No, he was still looking at that point on the horizon. At last he recovered himself. He spoke briefly to his lieutenant, then turned imperiously to me. "Professor, I now demand you obey one of the conditions of our bargain."

"What is that, Captain?"

"You must be confined, you and your companions, until I see fit to set you free again."

"You are the captain," I said, staring steadily at him, "but may I ask just one question?"

"No."

There was no resisting this attitude. I descended to Ned and Conseil's cabin and told them what had happened, and about the captain's demand. You can imagine how the Canadian took the news! But there was no time to take a stand. Four sailors waited at the door, and conducted us to that cell in which we had passed our first night on board. Ned put up some last-minute resistance, and then the door was shut on us.

Later, lunch was served. We ate in silence. Then the luminous globe went out and left us in darkness. Ned fell asleep and then, to my astonishment—for it was early in the day!—Conseil also fell into a heavy slumber. I was wondering what could have caused this drowsiness when I felt myself sinking into a stupor. Painful suspicion took hold of me. The food had been mixed with a strong sedative! Imprisonment was not enough to conceal Nemo's activities. Sleep was necessary too.

I could hear the hatches being closed. The undulations of the sea ceased. The *Nautilus* had submerged. I felt a mortal cold coming over my stiff, half-paralyzed limbs. My eyelids fell over my eyes like leaden seals. A morbid sleep, hallucinations, robbed me of my identity. Then even the visions vanished until, next morning, I woke with a perfectly clear head.

To my surprise, I was in my own cabin. I tried the door—it was unlocked—and I mounted the central stairs. The hatches were open again, and I went right out on the platform.

Ned and Conseil were waiting. I questioned them, but they were as ignorant of what had gone on during the night as I was. They too had been astonished to wake up in their own quarters.

And the *Nautilus* seemed as quiet and mysterious as ever.

Nothing seemed changed on board. With his powerful vision, Ned studied the ocean. It was deserted. Presently the lieutenant came out on deck and spoke his usual sentence to someone below.

About two p.m. I was in the salon, busy collating my notes, when the door opened and the captain entered. I greeted him. He bowed in response, but said nothing. I went on working, hoping he would explain what had happened. He seemed fatigued; his face looked profoundly sad. He walked up and down, sat, got up, picked up a book at random and then put it aside. Finally he came over to me. "Are you a physician, Monsieur Aronnax?"

It was such an unexpected question that for a moment I just stared. "Why yes," I said at last. "I am on the staff of the hospital. I practiced for years before I joined the museum."

"Good." Not knowing what to say next, I waited for him to follow through. "Monsieur Aronnax, would you be so good as to attend one of my men?"

"Of course."

"Come along then."

My heart beat wildly. I sensed a connection between this request and the events of the preceding day.

Captain Nemo led me to the poop and into a cabin near the sailors' quarters. On a bed lay a man about forty years old, a man with a resoluteness of expression that suggested to me that he was Anglo-Saxon. His head was swathed in bandages soaked in blood. As I undid the bandages, he looked at me with large eyes but gave no sign of any pain. It was a horrible wound. The skull had been hit by some blunt weapon, the brain was exposed. His breathing was slow, his face twitched, his pulse was intermittent. His extremities were already getting cold. I rebandaged his head and turned to the captain. "What caused this wound?" I demanded.

"What does it matter?" he replied. "A collision broke one of the pistons and it struck this man. The lieutenant was with him. He was flung down by the shock. A brother is to die for a brother, a friend for his friend, what could be simpler! That is the law for all on board the *Nautilus*. What are his chances?"

I hesitated.

"You can speak; he doesn't understand French."

"He will be dead in two hours."

"Nothing can save him?"

"Nothing."

The captain clenched his fists. Tears glistened in those eyes I had thought incapable of shedding tears.

I watched the dying man. He grew paler. I studied his intelligent forehead, furrowed with premature wrinkles. Perhaps his dying words would reveal the secret of his life. . . .

"You may go now, Professor," the captain said.

I left him at the man's bedside and returned to my own cabin, much disturbed. All day I was haunted by the incident. That night I slept badly. Between chaotic dreams, I thought I heard distant sighs, like the tones of a funeral chant.

As soon as I went out on the bridge in the morning the captain walked up to me. "Professor, can you and your friends go on an excursion today?"

"We obey your orders, Captain."

"Will you be so good, then, as to get into your diving suits?"

I sought out Ned and Conseil and told them about the captain's invitation. Conseil hastened to accept, and this time Ned seemed willing to go along. By half past eight we were fully equipped. The doors opened and, accompanied by Captain Nemo and a dozen or so of his crew, we stepped out onto the ocean floor.

A gradual declivity led us down to an uneven stretch, about fifteen fathoms deep. Turning on our Ruhmkorff lights, we followed a coral bank. Our route was bordered by thickets of shrub shapes covered with white starlike flowers. I saw some admirable specimens of rose coral; then I realized that I was in the Kingdom of the Corals! Chance had brought me into the presence of the most precious specimens of this zoophyte. Its tints deserve the poetic names "flower of blood" and "froth of blood" that commerce has given to these beautiful productions. Such coral sells for about one hundred dollars a pound, and these beds would have made the fortunes of a whole company of coral divers.

We continued walking downward, our lamps creating magical

effects as they played on the rough outlines of the coral arches and chandeliers. Two hours later we reached a depth of maybe three hundred yards, about the extreme limit at which coral can form. Here was an immense forest of huge petrified trees, tied by garlands of sea bindweed, all adorned with reflections and halos. We passed under high branches lost in the shade of the waves, while at our feet stars and meandrines formed a flowery carpet sprinkled with dazzling gems.

Captain Nemo had stopped. His men were forming a semicircle around him. Four of them, I noticed, were carrying on their shoulders an oblong object. We stood in the center of a vast glade surrounded by lofty foliage. Our lamps threw over the glade a sort of twilight that lengthened the shadows on the ground. It was darker at the end of the glade, where little points of coral seemed to throw off sparks. The ground was raised in certain places by mounds encrusted with limy deposits, arranged with a regularity that betrayed the hand of man. On a pedestal of rocks stood a coral cross. Its long arms seemed to be made of petrified blood. Ned and Conseil stood near me.

At a signal from Captain Nemo, a sailor stepped forward. A few feet from the cross he unhooked a pickaxe from his belt and began to dig a hole. This glade, then, was a cemetery, this hole a grave, that oblong object the body of the man who had died in the night! The sailor worked slowly. Fish fled on all sides. I saw the strokes of the pickaxe. It sparkled whenever it hit on some flint at the bottom of the waters.

Soon the hole was large enough. The four bearers approached. The corpse, wrapped in white byssus, was lowered into the wet grave. Captain Nemo and his companions, arms crossed over their chests, knelt in prayer. The debris torn from the sea floor was then thrown back on the tomb, forming a slight mound.

By one o'clock we had returned to the *Nautilus*. After changing my clothes, I went and sat on the platform, the victim of conflicting emotions. When Captain Nemo joined me, I stood up and said, "As I predicted, he died during the night?"

"Yes, Professor."

"And now he rests near his companions?"

"Yes, forgotten by everyone else, but not by us. We dig the grave, and the polyps seal our dead for eternity." Covering his face with his hands, he suppressed a sob. Then he added, "Our peaceful cemetery is here, hundreds of feet below the surface."

"Your dead sleep quietly, at least, beyond the reach of sharks."

"Yes, Professor," he responded, "of sharks and men."

X. THE INDIAN OCEAN

IN THE JANUARY DAYS that followed that moving scene in the coral graveyard, Conseil began to see the captain as an unappreciated genius who had repaid mankind's indifference with contempt and had taken refuge in the sea to exercise his talents freely. But to me, this hypothesis explained only one side of Captain Nemo. The mysteries of that night when we had been drugged; the captain's violent precaution in snatching the telescope from my hands; the mortal wound that that sailor had suffered from that unexplained collision—all these developments had put me on a new track. No! Captain Nemo was not satisfied with *shunning* humanity! His *Nautilus* served not only his instincts for freedom, but also perhaps his needs for a terrible vengeance!

But then I could not be sure. I could only catch glimpses of truth in all that darkness. I had to be content with recording what happened as the events themselves dictated.

We were now plowing the Indian Ocean, that vast liquid plain. Its waters are so clear, so transparent, that anyone leaning out over them actually feels giddy! To anyone but me, the hours without sight of land would have seemed long and monotonous. But walking on the platform, drinking in the stimulating sea air, studying the rich waters that passed the salon windows, reading in the library, working on my memoirs—these were pleasures which consumed all my time, leaving me not a moment for lassitude or ennui.

On the morning of January 24, in latitude 12° 5' south and

longitude 94° 33′ east, we sighted Keeling Island with its magnificent coconut trees. We skirted the shores of this desert island for a short distance. Our nets brought up numerous specimens of polypi, echinoderms and curious mollusks. Soon Keeling disappeared from the horizon, and we passed the Cocos Islands and turned northwest toward the Indian peninsula.

"India," Ned murmured. "Railroads, towns. Hindus, Englishmen, Frenchmen. How about it, Professor? Isn't it time to part company with Nemo?"

"Ned, we're probably heading for Europe. . . . Once there, we'll see what we can prudently do."

Deep down, I wanted to make best use of the good luck that had sent me on this undersea expedition. But, if luck also offered us a chance to escape, it would be cruel to sacrifice my companions to my passion for the unknown. The prisoner in me longed to escape, but the scientist in me still wanted to stay.

Two days later, we crossed the equator at the eighty-second meridian and reentered the northern hemisphere. On January 27 we were at the entrance to the Bay of Bengal, and there we saw corpses floating on the surface. They were the dead of the Indian towns, carried by the Ganges out to sea. The vultures, the only undertakers in that country, had not been able to devour them entirely. But now the sharks, the terrible creatures that multiply in those waters, helped them complete their funereal work.

When the *Nautilus* surfaced at noon on January 28, in latitude 9° 4′ north, I could see a range of mountains about eight miles to the west. We were nearing the island of Ceylon, the pearl that hangs from the lobe of the Indian peninsula.

Just then the captain appeared. "Ceylon is celebrated for its pearl fisheries! Would you like to visit one, Professor?"

"Certainly, Captain!"

"Good. I'll give orders that we head for the Gulf of Mannar. But even if we do see the fisheries, the best in the world, don't be disappointed if we can't see any fishermen. This is off-season for them. They will arrive in numbers during March. However, you and your companions will certainly be able to see the Mannar beds tomorrow, and if some fisherman just happens to be diving for pearls we'll watch him. Incidentally, are you afraid of sharks?"

"Sharks! I confess, Captain, I've never been intimate with that particular type of fish."

"But we know them well. So will you. However, we'll be well armed, and, on our way, who knows, we may take on a shark or two! It's good sport! So, until tomorrow morning, Professor!"

Now, when you're invited to hunt shark in its natural element, perhaps you should reflect before accepting. So reflect, I said to myself, wiping large drops of sweat from my forehead. Hunting otter in the forests of Crespo, that's one thing. But going deliberately where one is certain to encounter sharks, that's another thing. Sharks are quite capable of cutting a man in two. What a deplorable invitation! Maybe Conseil won't like to go—that would give me a good excuse for not accompanying the captain! But Ned Land—a man of his pugnacious nature may actually be attracted to it. . . .

Back in my cabin, I tried to concentrate on a book, but between the lines I kept seeing open-jawed sharks. When Conseil and Ned came in, they were calm, even happy. They had no idea what lay in wait for them. "Well, your Captain Nemo," Ned said, "has just made us a very pleasant offer!"

"Oh, you know about it?"

"If it is agreeable to the professor," Conseil interrupted, "the commander of the *Nautilus* invited us to visit the magnificent pearl fisheries tomorrow, in monsieur's company."

"That's all he said?"

"That's all, except that he had already spoken to you about this little jaunt." Ned seemed overjoyed.

"Would monsieur give us some information about pearl fishing?"

"About the fishing itself," I asked, "or about the . . . the er . . . circumstances . . . ?"

"About the fishing itself," Ned answered. "Just what is a pearl?"

"To a poet," I said, "a pearl is a teardrop of the sea. To the Orientals, it's a drop of dew solidified. To the ladies, it's a jewel of an oblong shape. To the chemist, it's a mixture of phosphate and carbonate of lime, with a little gelatin. For naturalists, finally, it is an abnormal growth formed over the years around a foreign body, maybe a sand grain, within the shell of certain mollusks. The mollusk par excellence that secretes the pearl is the pearl oyster."

"Can one find more than one pearl in the same oyster?" Conseil wanted to know.

"Yes, some oysters are like jewel boxes! I have heard about one oyster that contained a hundred and fifty sharks."

"A hundred and fifty *sharks!*" Ned exclaimed.

"Did I say sharks?" I cried out. "I meant to say a hundred and fifty pearls. Sharks wouldn't make sense."

"Of course not," Conseil said. "But would monsieur tell me if pearl fishing is dangerous?"

"Not if certain precautions are taken," I said hastily.

"What are the risks?" said Ned. "Swallowing salt water?"

"As you say, Ned. Incidentally"—I tried to assume Captain Nemo's careless tone—"are you afraid of sharks?"

"Me! A harpooner? It's my job to laugh at them!"

"But Ned, this is not a question of fishing for them with an iron swivel, hoisting them up on the ship, cutting off their tails, ripping them up, throwing their hearts overboard!"

"You mean it's a question . . ."

"Exactly. Down in the water."

"All I need is a good harpoon! You know, Professor, sharks are badly built. They must turn on their bellies to seize you, and by that time . . ."

The way he said "seize" made my blood run cold. "And Conseil, what do you think of sharks?"

"Me!" said Conseil. "I will be very frank. If monsieur faces the sharks, his faithful servant will be at his side!"

Sharks played an important part in my dreams that night. Finally I was awakened at four a.m. by the steward. I dressed in a hurry and went into the salon. The commander was waiting for me. "Ready to start, Professor?"

"All set, Captain."

"Then come along."

"Aren't we going to get into our diving suits?"

"Not yet. We're still quite a way from the Mannar beds. I can't let the *Nautilus* get too close to this coast. But the dinghy is ready, and our diving suits are in it. Rowing to the exact spot will save us a long walk."

I followed him up to the platform. Ned and Conseil, delighted to have a pleasure jaunt, were already there. Five sailors were in the dinghy, which had been made fast alongside. It was still dark. Layers of cloud obscured the stars.

We took our places in the stern of the dinghy. The painter was cast off and we headed south.

By six o'clock the sun's rays had pierced the curtain of clouds and I could see land distinctly, with trees scattered here and there. We were approaching Mannar Island, to the south. Captain Nemo stood up and was studying the sea.

At a signal from him the men dropped the anchor, but the chain scarcely ran. Here it was just about a yard deep. This was one of the high points of the oyster bank, which stretched more than twenty miles.

"We have arrived, Professor," the captain said. "Let's put on our diving suits and take a walk!"

I began with the help of the sailors to get into my heavy garments. Captain Nemo, Ned and Conseil were also being outfitted; but none of the *Nautilus*' men, apparently, were to go with us this time. Before putting my head into the copper helmet, I asked the captain about the Ruhmkorff lights.

"We are not going very deep, so the sun will give us all the light we need," he answered. "Besides, it would not be wise to carry electric lights into these waters. Their brilliance might attract the more dangerous inhabitants."

As he said this, I turned to Conseil and Ned, but they had already put on the helmets and could neither hear nor answer.

I had just one more question. "How about our guns?"

"Guns? What for? Mountaineers attack the bear with daggers. Isn't steel better than lead? Here is a knife! Put it in your belt."

I looked at my companions. They, too, were armed with knives, but Ned was also brandishing a huge harpoon. The captain and I got into our helmets. Once over the side, Captain Nemo gave the signal, and we trod on sand down a gentle declivity until we had disappeared under the water.

The fears that had obsessed me now vanished as the ease of my movements restored my confidence and the strangeness of the spectacle captured my imagination. Ten minutes later we were three fathoms down, on level terrain, where the tiniest object was clearly visible in the sunlight! Like coveys of snipe in a bog, shoals of fish rose at our feet, especially the genus monopteridae, which have no fins except their tails. I also recognized the Javanese, a real serpent almost a yard long, livid underneath, which could be mistaken for a conger eel if it were not for the gold stripes on its sides.

The rising sun lit the waters more and more. The soil changed little by little. After treading the fine sand we came to a perfect causeway of boulders, covered with carpets of mollusks and zoophytes. I saw some Purpura, or Thais, the kind that supplied purple dye for Captain Nemo; there were panopyres, slightly luminous, and oculines, like magnificent fans, one of the richest treelike growths of those seas.

At about seven o'clock we at last reached that part of the bank where pearl oysters reproduce by the millions; there were enormous heaps of them. Captain Nemo chose some of the finest specimens, removed the pearls and put them in a bag in his pocket.

But we did not stop for long. The Captain went on, seeming to be guided by paths known only to himself. The ground rose and fell, and often we rounded tall rocks scarped into pyramids. In their dark fissures were huge crustacea, poised on their high claws like some sort of war machine, watching us with fixed eyes. Then, quite suddenly, we entered a large grotto, formed by a picturesque heap of rocks, carpeted with thick submarine flora. My eyes became accustomed to the semidarkness. Arches sprang capriciously from natural pillars, standing broad on their granite base like heavy Tuscan columns. Why had our ever mysterious guide led us to the bottom of this underwater crypt?

Walking down a sharp declivity, we soon trod the bottom of a kind of circular pit. There Captain Nemo paused and pointed toward an oyster of extraordinary size, a gigantic tridacna seven feet wide! In awe I approached this fantastic mollusk. It adhered to a granite table by its byssus and there, alone, it was developing itself in the calm waters of this grotto! I reckoned its weight at about six hundred pounds. Such an oyster would contain thirty pounds of meat. Only a Gargantua would order a dozen!

Obviously Captain Nemo was acquainted with this bivalve, and seemed to have good reason to be checking on its condition. The shell was a bit open. The captain put his dagger between the halves to prevent them from closing. With his hand he lifted the fringed membrane that formed a cloak for this creature. There, between the pleats, I saw a loose pearl the size of a coconut! Its globular shape, perfect clarity and admirable luster made it a jewel of fantastic value. Carried away, I stretched out my hand to seize it, feel it. But the captain motioned no, and withdrew his dagger. The shell closed abruptly. Now I understood the captain's plan. He was letting the jewel grow. Each year the secretions of the mollusk would add new concentric layers. And already I could estimate its value to be at least ten million francs!

His visit to his opulent oyster at an end, Captain Nemo left the grotto, and we climbed again along the oyster bank. Suddenly the captain stopped and motioned to us to crouch beside him in a crevice in the rock. He pointed. About twenty feet away a shadow was sinking to the bottom. At first the disquieting thought of sharks shot through my mind, but I was wrong.

It was a man, a living man, an Indian fisherman, a poor devil who, no doubt, had come to gather *before* the harvest. I could see the bottom of his boat anchored about twenty feet above his head. He dived, went up, plunged again. Between his feet he held a stone, connected to his boat with a rope, which helped him descend more rapidly. Hitting bottom, he got on his knees and filled his bag with oysters snatched at random. Then he rose, emptied the bag, pulled up his stone and started over. Each trip took him about thirty seconds.

Because the rock hid us, he could not see us. I studied him. He worked with regularity; but for every oyster that contained a pearl I knew he would get only a penny, and I wondered how many of those oysters for which he was risking his life contained no pearls at all!

For half an hour, however, no danger threatened him. Then, just as I was beginning to take his safety for granted, I saw a gigantic shadow loom over him while he knelt on the bottom. It was a shark of huge dimensions, his eyes on fire, jaws open. He shot toward the Indian. The man tried to leap for the surface, but got entangled in his weighted rope. Although he flung himself to one side and avoided the shark's teeth, its tail hit his chest and stretched him out on the bottom.

The shark returned in a few seconds and, turning on its back, was getting ready to slice the Indian in half. Then Captain Nemo rose. Dagger in hand, he advanced toward the monster. Just as the shark was ready to snap the fisherman in two, he saw his new adversary, and, turning over, made straight for the captain.

I can still see Captain Nemo bracing himself, waiting calmly for the shark. When it lunged at him, he threw himself to one side with great nimbleness, avoiding the shock, and buried his dagger deep in its side. But it was not all over. A terrible combat ensued. If I may say so, the shark seemed to roar! Blood rushed in torrents from its wound. The sea was dyed red, and through the darkened waters I could see nothing more. Then, suddenly, I glimpsed the captain hanging on to a fin, struggling, it seemed, hand to hand with the shark, dealing blow on blow.

The shark's movements agitated the water so furiously that the rocking almost upset me. I wanted to fight by the captain's side, but I confess I was rooted to the spot with horror. A moment later I saw the captain fall. The shark's jaws opened like a pair of metal shears, and it would have been all over for the captain when, quick as thought, Ned Land rushed at the shark and struck it with his harpoon. The sea was clouded with yet more blood as the shark beat the water with indescribable rage. But Ned had struck it to the heart. It was the monster's death rattle.

Apparently unhurt, the captain went straight for the Indian, cut the rope that held him to the stone, lifted him in his arms, and with a sharp push mounted to the surface. The whole episode had taken only a few moments. We all followed, up to the fisherman's boat.

The captain's first thought was to revive the unlucky man. I did not think it could be done. But Conseil and the captain both worked vigorously over him, and the diver slowly regained consciousness. He opened his eyes. What was his surprise, even his panic, at seeing four immense copper heads leaning over his boat! What must he have thought when Captain Nemo pulled the bag of pearls from his pocket and put them in the diver's hands! Trembling, the poor man accepted this magnificent charity, but his gaping eyes showed that he did not know what superhuman creatures to thank for his fortune and his life.

At a signal from the captain, we returned to the oyster bank. In about half an hour we reached the anchor of the dinghy. Once aboard, we got out of the helmets with the help of the sailors. Captain Nemo's first word was for Ned. "Thank you, Master Land."

"It was tit for tat, Captain," Ned replied. "I owed you that."

A pale smile passed over the captain's features. That was all. "Back to the *Nautilus*," he said.

The boat flew over the waves and a few minutes later we met the floating body of the dead shark. By the black marking on the fins, I could identify it as the terrible melanopteron. It was more than twenty-five feet long, and its mouth occupied a third of its body. While we were staring at it, a dozen of its fellows surfaced near our boat, flung themselves on the corpse and fought viciously among themselves for every shred.

By eight thirty a.m. we were back on board our ship. There I reflected on our adventures at the Mannar bank. Inevitably I had to come to two conclusions. Captain Nemo was a man of unparalleled courage. And he could still show concern for a human being, a member of that race from which he himself had fled. Whatever he might say, this strange man had not succeeded in killing his own heart.

When I mentioned this to him, he replied with some feeling, "That Indian, Professor, lives in the land of the oppressed! I am now—and even to my last breath will still be—also one of the oppressed!"

XI. THE ARABIAN TUNNEL

ON JANUARY 29, the island of Ceylon disappeared below the horizon. We had traveled 7500 French leagues, or 16,220 miles, from our point of departure in the Sea of Japan. Our course was northwest, in the direction of the Red Sea, and that was a dead end, with no exit! Where was Captain Nemo taking us? I, for one, had no idea. But this would not satisfy the Canadian, who came to me that day to get information about our destination.

"We go where the captain's fancy takes us," I said.

"Then his fancy can't take us far. If we enter the Red Sea, we'll come out again before long, for the Suez Canal is not yet completed. In short, the Red Sea is not the way that leads to Europe!"

"I never said we're going to Europe."

"What do you suppose we're doing, then?"

"I suppose that after visiting the exotic coasts of Arabia and Egypt, the *Nautilus* will go down the Indian Ocean again, so as to gain the Cape of Good Hope."

"And once we're at the Cape of Good Hope . . . ?"

"Well, we could sail into the Atlantic, which we haven't yet visited. Ah, Ned, I know you're bored with all these undersea marvels. As for me, I will greatly regret the end of this voyage that it has been given to so few men to make. But the end will come. Discussion is useless for the present. If you were to come to me and say, 'I see here a good chance to escape,' then I would discuss that with you. But such is not the case. And I do not believe the captain will venture into European waters."

On February 5 we entered the Gulf of Aden, a perfect funnel introduced into the neck of Bab el Mandeb, through which the Indian waters enter the Red Sea. The following day, I caught a glimpse of Aden's octagonal minarets. I certainly expected that Captain Nemo would back out at this point. But, much to my surprise, he did no such thing. And on February 7 we entered the Strait of Bab el Mandeb, which means, in Arabic, "The Gate of Tears." But I did not see it. There were too many French and English ships in this narrow passage for the *Nautilus* to show herself above the surface. At last, about midday, we entered the Red Sea.

I would not even try to understand the caprice that had led Captain Nemo to enter the Red Sea. But I quite enjoyed our being there. We slowed down sometimes to avoid a ship, and so I was able to study the upper and the lower strata of this curious sea.

In the early hours of February 8, we approached the African shore, where the sea is much deeper. Through the open panels we contemplated the beautiful shrubs of brilliant coral, and the sponges and plants of all shapes that grew there, pediculated, foliated, globular, digital. They deserve the names of elkhorn, lion's foot, peacock's-tail, Neptune's cup, which the fishermen, who dredge them up or dive for them, have given them. The fish were abundant. In the nets of the *Nautilus* we caught brick-red rays and whiptail stingrays; fiatoles, a species of Stromateidae with gold bands and trimmed with the three colors of France; mullets with yellow heads; triggerfish, and a thousand other species common to those waters.

On February 9 the *Nautilus* sailed the broadest part of the Red Sea, between Suakin, on the west coast, and al-Qunfidha on the east, almost two hundred miles apart. After the bearings were taken at noon, Captain Nemo mounted to the platform. I was determined not to let him descend until I had a chance to talk to him about his long-range plans. He graciously offered me a cigar.

"Well, Professor, have you observed the wonders of the Red Sea?"

"Yes, Captain. The *Nautilus* is wonderfully fitted for such observations. The ancients, if I recall correctly, regarded it as a dangerous, detestable sea. It is clear that they never sailed on the *Nautilus*."

"Without a doubt." He smiled. "And yet, moderns are not

really so much more advanced than the ancients. It may take another hundred years before there is a second *Nautilus*. Progress is very slow, Professor."

"Your boat is at least a century before its time. What a misfortune if its secrets should perish with its inventor!"

The captain did not reply to that directly, but said, "You were talking of the opinions of the ancients. Even they understood the importance of a connection between the Red Sea and the Mediterranean. You have a right to be proud of your countryman, Monsieur de Lesseps, for attempting what they did not dare attempt. Such a man brings more glory to a nation than its great soldiers. All honor to Monsieur de Lesseps!"

"All honor to a great citizen!" I replied, surprised by Captain Nemo's manner.

"Unfortunately, Professor, I cannot take you through his Suez Canal, as it will not be completed until next year. But you will be able to see the long jetties of Port Said the day after tomorrow, when we will enter the Mediterranean."

"Enter the Mediterranean!" I exclaimed.

"Yes, sir. Why does that astonish you?"

"What astonishes me is the speed you'll have to travel, to go around Africa, to be in the Mediterranean the day after tomorrow!"

"Who told you we'd go around Africa?"

"Well, unless you sail over dry land, over the isthmus . . ."

"Or *beneath* it, Professor."

"Beneath it!"

"Of course," he replied quietly. "A long time ago nature made, under this tongue of land, what man is now making on its surface—a subterranean passage that I call the Arabian Tunnel. It takes us beneath Suez and into the Bay of Pelusium."

"But this isthmus is composed of nothing but shifting sands!"

"To a certain depth. Just a hundred and sixty feet down there is solid rock."

"Did you discover this passage by chance?"

"By reasoning more than by chance. I noticed that in the Red Sea and in the Mediterranean there are many identical fishes—

phidia, fiatoles, *girelles*—so I asked myself, Could there be a connection between the two seas? If so, the subterranean current would have to run from the Red Sea to the Mediterranean, because of the difference in their level. I caught a large number of these fishes near Suez. I put copper rings in their tails and tossed them back into the sea. Months later, I caught some of them again, off Syria. Thus I established the connection. I went looking for it with my *Nautilus*. Before long, Professor, you too will have traveled through my Arabian Tunnel."

When I passed on this news to my companions, Conseil clapped his hands, but the Canadian just shrugged his shoulders.

"A submarine tunnel connecting two seas!" he cried. "Whoever heard of such a thing!"

"But Ned," responded Conseil, "whoever heard of a *Nautilus*? It exists anyhow! You can't reject things just because you never heard of them!"

Next morning, February 10, we sighted several ships running on our opposite tack, and we were obliged to return to the depths. But at midday, when we took our bearings, the sea was deserted, so we stayed on the surface. The coast to the east looked like something faintly printed on a damp fog. We were leaning against the small boat, talking of this and that, when suddenly Ned pointed out to sea and said, "Do you see something right there, Professor?"

"No, Ned, but I don't have eyes like yours!"

"Look there, on the starboard beam."

"I see it now. Like a long black body on the surface."

"Another *Nautilus?*" Conseil suggested.

"No. I may be wrong, but I think it's an animal! However, it's not a whale."

"We need only be patient," Conseil said. "We'll soon know."

Indeed, it wasn't more than a mile away now.

"It moved! Look, it's diving!" Ned suddenly cried. "A thousand devils! What kind of animal is it? Its fins are like—stumps of legs!"

"Then maybe . . ." I wondered.

"Say," Ned went on, "she's rolled over, with her breasts in the air!"

"A mermaid!" Conseil guessed.

That cinched it for me. "Not a mermaid," I said, "but a rare species that has provided the popular imagination with fables about mermaids. Only a few specimens survive in the Red Sea. It's a dugong."

Ned's eyes blazed with excitement. He looked as if he might actually jump overboard and fight the animal in its native element!

Captain Nemo came out on the platform, spotted the dugong, and sized up the situation. "If you had a harpoon," he said to Ned, "it would burn your fingers."

"That's right, sir!" the Canadian answered.

"You'd like to be back at your old trade?"

"Oh, yes, sir!"

"Go ahead, add that dugong to your list of trophies. But I advise you, don't miss."

"Why?" I asked. "Is it dangerous to attack a dugong?"

"Oh yes," the captain said. "Sometimes it turns on its attackers and upsets their boat. But that's not a real danger for Master Land. His arm is strong. I advise him not to miss because the dugong is a superb dish, and I know that Master Land does not dislike a tasty morsel."

"You mean it's good to eat too!" Ned exclaimed.

"It's a dish reserved for princes of the East."

In a few minutes, seven sailors, impassive as ever, mounted the platform. One carried a harpoon and line. They let the dinghy down into the sea. Six took places at the oars, and the seventh went to the tiller. Ned, Conseil and I sat in the stern.

"Aren't you coming, Captain?" I asked.

"Not this time. But I wish you good sport!"

The dinghy moved quickly toward the dugong. Several cable lengths from the animal, the sailors slowed down, dipping their oars gently into the quiet waters. Harpoon in hand, Ned stood forward. The harpoon used for striking a whale is usually attached to a long rope that runs out quickly as the wounded animal pulls it with him. But here, I noticed, the rope was not more than ten fathoms long, and the end was attached to a small barrel. Floating on the surface, this barrel would show the direction the dugong was taking underwater.

I studied the animal carefully. The dugong's oblong body terminates in a long tail and its lateral fins in fingers. Its upper jaw is armed with two long, diverging tusks. This particular dugong was colossal in size; it was twenty feet or more in length. It seemed to be sleeping on the waves.

Now we were only fifteen feet from this silent mass! The oars rested in the oarlocks. Ned, leaning back, brandished his weapon in his expert hand. We heard a hissing sound. The dugong disappeared. It looked as if the harpoon had hit nothing but water.

"A thousand devils!" Ned screamed. "I missed!"

"No, Ned," I shouted. "Look at all the blood! But your harpoon didn't stick."

"My harpoon!" Ned cried. "My harpoon!"

The sailors leaned on the oars and the mate steered for the barrel. Recovering his harpoon, Ned was set for another blow. Now and then the animal surfaced for air, but apparently it was not much weakened by the wound, for it always dived again. Without rest, we pursued it for an hour. I was about to despair of our ever capturing it when—apparently seized with the idea of vengeance—the animal suddenly came to within a few feet of the boat.

"Be careful now!" Ned shouted.

The dugong paused, sniffed, and—flung itself upon us.

We could not avoid the shock. Almost upset, we must have shipped at least two tons of water. Ned clung to the bow and belabored the creature with his harpoon. The dugong fastened its teeth on our gunwale and raised us as a lion lifts a deer. We fell over each other in the boat. I don't know how it would have ended if Ned had not finally found the heart of the beast with his sharp point. I heard its teeth grinding on the iron gunwale, and then the dugong disappeared, taking the harpoon with her. But the barrel soon bobbed to the surface, and then the body of the animal surfaced too. We took it in tow and headed for the *Nautilus*.

They used tackle of enormous strength to hoist the dugong up onto the platform. It must have weighed five tons. That very evening, the steward served me choice cuts of dugong flesh. I found it excellent, superior to beef and even to veal.

The next afternoon, the *Nautilus* passed into the Strait of Jubal, which leads into the Gulf of Suez. I could see Mount Horeb, or Sinai, at whose summit Moses had met God face-to-face. The waters around us were tinted red by millions of microscopic plants known as trichodesmia, and I could well understand the origin of the name Red Sea.

We sailed after that below the surface and then came up again at nine fifteen p.m. Mounting the platform, I could see a pale light, partly obscured by fog, shining about a mile away.

"The floating lighthouse of Suez," said the captain, appearing at my elbow. "Soon we shall be at the entrance of the tunnel."

"It must be difficult to enter."

"Yes, that's why I stay in the steersman's cage and direct the operation myself. If you will be so good as to descend now, Monsieur Aronnax, the *Nautilus* is about to submerge." He led me halfway down the central staircase and then along to the pilot's cage, which stood at the forward end of the platform. It was a cabin about six feet square, similar to the pilot's cabins on the Mississippi and Hudson riverboats. In the center was the wheel, placed vertically and connected to the tiller rope, which ran to the stern. As soon as my eyes adjusted to the darkness I could see the helmsman, a strong man, his hands on the spokes. The sea around us was vividly illuminated by our searchlight, which shed its rays from the other end of the platform, behind us.

"Now for the tunnel," said the captain. He pressed a button connected with the engine room, and at once the propeller slowed down. For an hour we ran alongside a high wall that formed the solid base of a massive sandy coast. Captain Nemo kept his eye on the compass. Repeatedly, at a signal from the captain, the helmsman would make some small adjustment in our course.

At ten fifteen p.m. Captain Nemo took the wheel himself. A large, black, deep gallery opened before us and the *Nautilus* plunged boldly into it. I heard a strange roaring along our sides. It was the waters of the Red Sea, pouring through the inclined tunnel down toward the Mediterranean. The *Nautilus* went along with the torrent, swift as an arrow, although the captain was cutting our speed by running the engines in reverse!

On the tunnel walls I saw a continuous pattern of brilliant rays, straight furrows of fire, traced by our searchlight. I could feel my heart beating fast.

At ten thirty-five Captain Nemo left the wheel.

"The Mediterranean Sea!" he announced to me.

In less than twenty minutes the *Nautilus*, swept along by the torrent, had passed under the Isthmus of Suez.

XII. ACROSS THE MEDITERRANEAN

WHEN THE *Nautilus* surfaced at dawn the next day, February 12, I rushed out onto the platform. Ned and Conseil joined me. Those inseparable companions had been sleeping peacefully, unconcerned with the *Nautilus'* great feat!

"Well, Sir Naturalist," the Canadian demanded in a jovial tone, "where's the Mediterranean?"

"You're sailing on it, Ned."

"What! Right now? I don't believe it."

"Then see how wrong you are, Ned. With your good eyes, can't you see those jetties of Port Said?"

He looked at them carefully. "Actually," he said, "you're right, Professor, and your captain is a masterful man! So we *are* in the Mediterranean! Listen, then, let us talk now of our private affairs— someplace where no one will overhear us."

I knew of course what he wanted, and I felt it was better for him to get it off his chest. We all sat down near the searchlight. "Go ahead, Ned."

"It's very simple. Here we are in Europe. Before the captain's whims drag us down to the South Pole or to Oceania, I want to leave the *Nautilus*."

I could see that this talk was going to be embarrassing for me. I certainly did not want to limit the freedom of my companions, but

This glade, then, was a cemetery, this hole a grave, that oblong object the body of the man who had died in the night!

Our course was northwest, in the direction of the Red Sea, and that was a dead end, with no exit!

Ned clung to the bow and belabored the creature with his harpoon.

Captain Nemo was there, bent over his organ.

The Nautilus was stationary, floating on a lake, imprisoned by a circle of walls about two miles in diameter.

Beyond the Nautilus' spur lay a frozen plain.

But who could have saved him from that terrible hug? Captain Nemo nevertheless flung himself at the squid and sliced off another tentacle.

But when I did regain consciousness, I was lying in a fisherman's hut in the Norwegian Lofoten Islands.

I personally had no desire at all to leave Captain Nemo. Thanks to him I was rewriting my book on the submarine depths. I would never again have such an opportunity! I could not bring myself to leave before my research was completed.

"I've told you, Ned, that this journey will come to an end—probably in six months, when the seas have nothing more in store for us."

"And where shall we be in six months, Sir Naturalist?"

"Maybe in China. But we may have chances to escape off France, England, America."

"Monsieur Aronnax, your arguments are rotten at the core. You speak in the future. 'We shall be there! We shall be here!' I speak in the present. We are here and we must take advantage of it!"

I felt beaten; I could think of no new arguments!

"Professor," Ned continued, "if Captain Nemo made you an offer never to be renewed, to let you go free, right now, would you accept it?"

"I do not know."

"And what do you think, Conseil?" Ned demanded.

"Conseil," Conseil replied, "is absolutely disinterested in the question. Conseil is in the service of his master, he thinks like his master, he speaks like his master."

"Well, Professor," said Ned, "since Conseil does not exist at all, the discussion is between you and me. I have spoken. What's your position?"

"Ned, you're right, I suppose. I know we must not rely on Captain Nemo's goodwill. Common sense forbids him to set us free. On the other hand, common sense says we must take the first good opportunity to escape. But, Ned, our first attempt must be well thought out. If it fails, we shall never have another chance. Captain Nemo will see to that."

"But we agree: if a good chance presents itself, we seize it!"

"Agreed! Now, Ned, what is a good chance?"

"One that brings the *Nautilus* close to some European shore. If she happened to be on the surface, I would try to escape by swimming. If she were underwater, I would try to get control of the dinghy. We can get into the dinghy, take out the bolts and shoot up to the surface. Not even the pilot—he's up forward there—would know."

"Well, Ned, watch for that good chance. When you are ready, let us know and we shall follow you. I rely entirely on you. But would you like to know what I really think of the plan?"

"Of course, Professor."

"I think your good chance will never present itself. Captain Nemo surely realizes that we still hope for freedom. He will always be on his guard, especially in European waters."

"Well"—Ned shook his head in a determined way—"we'll see."

During the following day, to his great despair, the facts seemed to confirm my foresight. Did Captain Nemo distrust us in those well-traveled seas? Or did he merely wish to hide from the numerous ships that plowed the Mediterranean? I could not say. But more frequently we were underwater, more frequently away from the coasts. When we did come to the surface, we could see nothing.

Next day, February 14, I resolved to spend some time studying the fishes of the region. But for some reason or other, the panels never opened. Taking our bearings, I discovered that we were approaching Candia, the ancient isle of Crete. When I had embarked on the *Abraham Lincoln*, this island had been in revolt against the despotism of the Turks. How the rebels had fared since then I could not tell. Captain Nemo, I thought, would be unable to tell me, since he was cut off from all communication with the land. And so, when I found myself alone with him in the salon that night, I didn't even mention the Greek rebellion. He said very little and seemed to be thinking a great deal. Contrary to his habit, he now had both panels opened and, stalking from one to the other, kept looking into the waters. I took advantage of the chance to study my fishes. I noticed some gobies, mentioned by Aristotle, commonly known as sea loaches. Near them rolled some semiphosphorescent snappers, a kind of sparus which the ancient Egyptians considered sacred; their arrival in the Nile announced the flood season.

Suddenly, out there, a man appeared, with a leather purse at his belt! He was swimming with strong strokes, rising occasionally to the surface to breathe, plunging down again.

I turned to the captain and exclaimed: "A shipwrecked man! We must save him!"

Saying nothing, the captain leaned against the glass. The man had flattened his face against the window and was looking at us. To my astonishment, Captain Nemo signaled to him, and the man answered with his hand. He shot immediately to the surface and did not return.

"Don't be upset," Captain Nemo said. "That's Nicholas of Cape Matapan, well known in all the Cyclades. A hardy diver! The water is his home. He lives in it more than on land, going incessantly from one island to the next, even as far as Crete."

"Then you know him well, Captain?"

"And why not, Professor?"

So saying, he walked toward a bureau standing near the left panel of the salon. Next to this bureau was a chest bound with iron, covered with a copper plate on which was engraved *Mobilis in mobili*. Ignoring me, the captain opened the bureau, which, it developed, contained a great many ingots.

Ingots of gold! A fortune in precious metal! Where, I wondered, did he get these riches, and what was he going to do with them? But I kept mum. I watched the captain take out ingots, one by one, and arrange them methodically in the chest, until he had filled it to the top. That coffer, I estimated, must have held a ton of gold, almost five million francs!

He fastened the chest securely and wrote an address on the lid in characters that looked to me like modern Greek. Then he pressed a button. Four men entered and, with considerable strain, they pushed the chest out of the salon. I heard them arranging pulleys to hoist it up the central staircase.

"And," the captain turned to me, "you were saying, Professor?"

"I was saying nothing, Captain."

"Well, then excuse me, and I wish you good night."

Much disturbed, I returned to my cabin. I tried in vain to sleep. I was thinking of the relationship between the appearance of this diver and the coffer filled with gold. Soon, I could tell by our rolling movements, we were leaving the depths and mounting to the surface. I heard the sound of steps on the platform. I knew they were launching the dinghy. It banged once on the hull, and then all sounds ceased.

Two hours later, similar noises. The dinghy, hoisted on board, was fitted into its socket, and the *Nautilus* submerged. So, the millions had been delivered to their address! To what point on the Continent? Who was the captain's contact on land?

Next morning, I told Ned and Conseil about these nocturnal doings, and they were just as puzzled as I. The following dawn, February 16, we left the basin between Rhodes and Alexandria and, having doubled Cape Matapan, quitted the Greek archipelago.

The Mediterranean, the blue sea beyond compare! Known to the Greeks as "the sea," to the Romans as "our sea"! Bordered with orange trees, aloes, sea pines; saturated with pure, transparent air! But, beautiful as it was, I could take only quick looks at its eight hundred thousand square miles of blue water. Even Captain Nemo's special knowledge of it was lost to me, for that inexplicable person appeared not even once during our rapid crossing.

It seemed evident that he disliked the Mediterranean, enclosed by those very countries he wanted most to avoid. Those waters, those winds perhaps brought back too many memories, if not regrets. And here he did not enjoy that liberty of movement that he loved so much in the open seas. Doubtless he felt crowded between the close shores of Africa and Europe.

To his great disgust poor Ned now had to abandon all his plans for escape. He could not launch the dinghy, since we now averaged twenty-five knots, or thirty-five to forty feet a second! The *Nautilus* surfaced only at night to replenish her air supply, and so we glimpsed the Mediterranean through the panels, the way passengers on an express train see the landscape that blurs past the windows.

On the night of February 16, we slowed down to pass between Sicily and Tunis. In this channel the sea bottom rose almost abruptly to form a perfect bank, about nine fathoms deep. On the other side we entered the second Mediterranean basin, fifteen hundred fathoms deep in some spots. Using the diving planes, the captain drove the boat into its lowest depths. There the waters offered to the view terrible and moving scenes. From the Algerian coast to the shores of Provence, so many shipwrecks, so many lost warships! The sea is strewn with anchors, cannon, propellers, pistons, smokestacks.

Swift and indifferent, the *Nautilus* ran at full speed through this museum of ruins, and at dawn on February 18 we passed through the Strait of Gibraltar. A few minutes later we floated out on the Atlantic.

I estimated that we had traveled six hundred leagues in forty-eight hours.

XIII. THE ATLANTIC

As soon as she had left the Mediterranean the *Nautilus* surfaced. At the first opportunity, accompanied by Ned and Conseil, I went up to the platform to look at the Atlantic. The *Nautilus* was cutting its waters after logging nearly ten thousand leagues in three and a half months. And where were we heading now, what did the future hold in store for us?

We could barely make out, about twelve miles away, Cape Saint Vincent, the southwestern point of the Iberian Peninsula. A strong southerly gale was blowing, and we found it difficult to keep our footing on the platform. Quickly gulping down some fresh air, we went below again. Conseil went to his cabin but the Canadian followed me to my quarters. Our rapid crossing of the Mediterranean had thwarted his plans for escape, and he could not hide his disappointment. Closing the door of my cabin, he sat down and stared silently at me.

"Ned," I said, "it would have been foolhardy to attempt escape under those conditions."

He did not answer, but his lips tightened.

"We don't have to give up yet," I added. "We seem to be going up the Portuguese coast. France and England lie ahead, and we could find refuge there. Probably in just a few days you can act with certainty."

He still looked at me in that fixed way. At last his lips moved and he said, "It's all set for tonight."

I stood up involuntarily. I admit I was surprised. I wanted to answer him but words just wouldn't come.

"We agreed to wait for a good chance," he continued, "and the good chance is now. Tonight we'll still be close to the Iberian coast, and there's a good wind. I have your promise, Professor. I count on it."

Perhaps because I still did not answer, he came closer. "Tonight at nine," he said. "I've already alerted Conseil. At that time Captain Nemo will be in his room. Conseil and I will go up the central staircase. You must stay in the library and wait for my signal. I've checked the dinghy. I've even managed to stow away a little food in her. We're all set."

"The sea is bad," I said.

"I admit that, but liberty is worth the risk. And remember, by tomorrow the *Nautilus* could be a hundred leagues from any shore! But let's just have a little luck tonight, and by midnight we shall land on terra firma. Until tonight, then, adieu."

I had imagined that, after losing our chance in the Mediterranean, I would have a little time to reflect. Now I was dumbfounded. Ned was gone. He had given me no time to consider. But after all, what could I have said? I could not go back on my word.

I heard a loud hissing: the tanks were filling. The *Nautilus* was submerging.

I stayed in my cabin, packing my notes. I wanted to avoid the captain, who would surely notice that I was upset. It was a sad day for me. I wanted to be free again, but I also wanted to complete my research, to discover the secrets of the Atlantic as I had discovered the secrets of the Pacific and Indian oceans. Sometimes I caught myself hoping that something would prevent Ned from giving that signal! But I had to do my part, even though I wondered what Captain Nemo would think. Would he be hurt by my escape? Would I see him again before we left?

The hours passed slowly. At last the steward served my dinner in my cabin, and I ate. One hundred and twenty minutes—I reckoned the time that way—still separated me from that moment when I was to join Ned. I realized that failure in itself did not disturb me—what did disturb me was the thought of being caught in the act of escape, being brought before the captain, who would be irritated, maybe even disillusioned by my desertion—the thought of that painful confrontation made my heart beat hard.

I wanted one last look around the salon. I wandered through the museum, where I had spent so many agreeable hours. I reviewed all its treasures, like a man on the verge of eternal exile. I wanted most of all to take a last fond look at those submarine depths, the greatest privilege of all on this unprecedented journey. But the panels were closed! A curtain of steel kept me from that ocean I had not yet begun to explore.

To my great surprise, the door to the captain's room was slightly ajar. I drew back, afraid that he might see me. But hearing no sound at all, I looked in and saw that the room was deserted. It still had that same monklike severity, but suddenly I noticed something I had never seen before—watercolors on the far wall. They were portraits of great men who had devoted their lives to the advancement of humanity: Kosciusko, the champion of Polish independence; O'Connell, the defender of Ireland; Washington, the founder of the American Union; Manin, the Italian patriot. What spiritual tie did Captain Nemo feel with these heroes? Would this tie explain the mystery of his life? Was he also a fighter for oppressed peoples, a liberator of enslaved races?

The clock struck eight. The first stroke startled me from my reverie, and I hurried out of the captain's room. Returning to my cabin, I dressed in my seaboots, my otterskin cap, my byssus overcoat. At a few moments to nine, I walked through the partly lighted but deserted salon to the library. The same low light, the same solitude.

I took my place near the door leading to the central staircase and waited for Ned's signal. Then the vibrations of the propeller stopped! The silence was broken only by the beating of my own heart. I felt a slight shock, and I knew from experience that it meant we were resting on the ocean floor. My anxiety grew. Ned's signal did not come. Instead, the door opened and Captain Nemo appeared!

"I've been looking for you!" he said. "Do you know Spanish history?"

Now, you may know the history of a country by heart. Yet in the condition I was in at that moment, I would not have been able to recite a bit of it.

"Well, Professor, didn't you hear my question? Do you know Spanish history?"

"Not very well," I said.

"Sit down then and I shall recount for you an episode from that history." He sat on a divan and, mechanically, I sat next to him in the half-light. "It will interest you for at least one reason. It will answer a big question that has doubtless puzzled you."

"I'm listening." What was he driving at? Did this have something to do with our plans for flight?

"Let us go back to 1702, when your king, Louis the Fourteenth, had imposed his grandson, the Duke of Anjou, on the Spanish. This prince reigned more or less poorly under the title of Philip the Fifth. Opposition to his rule grew: Holland, Austria and England concluded a treaty with the intention of lifting the crown from his head. Spain had to fight this coalition. She was almost without army or navy, but money in abundance was on the way, galleons from America, laden with gold and silver.

"Near the end of 1702 this rich convoy was expected to arrive at Cadiz, with a French escort of twenty-three warships commanded by Admiral Chateau-Renaud. But the admiral heard that the English were patrolling that area and he was foolishly persuaded, by the Spanish commanders in his convoy, to make for Vigo Bay, on the northwest coast of Spain. Unhappily, Vigo Bay was militarily untenable.

"On October 22, 1702, the English fleet arrived, and although he was outnumbered, Admiral Renaud fought bravely. When he saw that the treasure would fall into enemy hands, he burned and scuttled every galleon. They went to the bottom with their immense wealth." He paused.

"So?" I asked, not seeing the relationship to me.

"Well, Professor, we are now in Vigo Bay. Are you interested in looking into its secrets?"

He got up, suggesting that I follow him. I had had time to recover. The salon was dark, but the panels now opened, and through the glass I could see the sea for half a mile around us, bathed in electric light. Some of our crew, wearing diving suits, were lifting barrels and chests out of a blackened shipwreck and carrying them back to the *Nautilus*. From these barrels and chests escaped ingots of silver and gold, cascades of jewels and coins. The sands were piled high with them. And now I understood! Whenever Captain Nemo needed money, he came to pick up these millions from the sunken galleons. He was sole heir to the wealth of the Incas, the loot of Cortez.

"Professor, did you ever dream that the seas held so much wealth?"

"I know it is estimated that there are two million tons of silver held in suspension in seawater. I pity the thousands of poor people to whom this wealth could have been a bonanza. For them these riches will remain forever buried." I had no sooner expressed this regret than I realized that I must have offended Captain Nemo.

"Forever buried! Do you think, sir, that these riches are forever lost because *I* gather them? Do you think I take the trouble to collect these treasures for myself alone? Do you think I do not know there are suffering, oppressed peoples on this earth, miserable victims to be helped, to be avenged? How can you be so blind?"

He stopped at these last words, perhaps sorry that he had uttered so many. But I knew now that whatever motive had led him to seek independence under the sea, he was still a human being. His heart still beat for suffering humanity, his immense charity was available for oppressed groups as well as for unfortunate individuals. And I could guess who had received those millions, that night when the *Nautilus* was sailing off insurgent Crete.

NEXT MORNING, AS I HAD EXPECTED, the Canadian came to my room, looking terribly disappointed.

"Luck was against us, Ned, that's all," I said.

"That confounded captain had to stop at the very moment we were going to jump his ship!"

"Well, Ned, he had some business with his bank."

"His bank!"

I told him what had happened the night before, with the secret hope of interesting him in staying on board a while longer. But my tale only excited his regrets that he had not been able to loot those wrecks himself.

"We're not finished, though," he said. "I've failed once, but tonight . . ."

"What direction are we heading now?"

"I don't know," Ned admitted.

"Well, we'll get our bearings at noon."

About eleven thirty we surfaced. I rushed out to the platform, but not before Ned could get there. No land in sight! At noon the lieutenant took his bearings. Then the sea grew rough and we descended. An hour later I saw our position marked on the chart. We were a hundred and fifty leagues from the nearest land, and our course was south-southwest! I leave you to imagine the fury of the Canadian, but I admit that I personally was relieved. I buried myself happily in my work.

It must have been eleven p.m. when Captain Nemo suddenly appeared and asked me very graciously whether I was tired from my observations of the night before. I assured him that I had survived.

"Well, then, Professor, I suggest a novel excursion. So far you have walked on the ocean floor only in the daytime. How would you like to visit the submarine depths at night?"

"Yes, I would like that."

"I warn you, we have a long hike, and must climb a mountain."

"You're only building up my curiosity. I am all set to go."

In the dressing room, I saw that neither my companions nor any member of the crew were to go along on this trip. In a few moments they were putting the reservoirs on our backs, but they had not prepared any electric lamps for us. I pointed this out to the captain.

"We don't need them," he replied.

I thought I had not heard correctly, but I could not repeat my question because the captain's head was already encased in metal. Just before we went into the intermediate chamber they put an iron walking stick into my hand, and then we set foot on the Atlantic bottom.

It was almost midnight. The water was profoundly dark, but Captain Nemo pointed to a red glow about two miles away. What this illumination could be I could not say, but it did light our way. I could hear a pattering over my head. The noise intensified, some-times to become a loud crackling. I soon discovered that it was rain falling violently on the surface of the ocean. Instinctively the thought crossed my mind that I would get wet! In the water! I could not help laughing inside my helmet at this bizarre idea.

Half an hour later I could feel the bottom becoming stony. Medusae, microscopic crustacea and pennatulas lit it with their faint phosphorescence, giving me glimpses of a carpet formed by millions of zoophytes and masses of seaweed. I often slipped on this carpet, and without my iron walking stick I would have tumbled several times. Turning around, I could see the *Nautilus'* searchlight fading in the distance. And the rosy light that guided us was growing brighter. The glimmering seemed to come from behind a distant mountain peak about eight hundred feet high.

It was about one a.m. when we approached the first slopes of this mountain. But to cross them we had to find our way through a vast forest. Yes, a forest of dead trees with no leaves and no sap, petrified by the action of the water! Their underparts were somber, the upper tinted red by the light. I walked boldly across extended trunks, breaking the sea bindweed slung from one tree to the next, frightening the fish that flew from branch to limb. Ever climbing, we loosened stones that tumbled behind us with the enormous leaps and growls of an avalanche.

I was following an indefatigable leader; and I could not lag behind, so I pushed on with my iron stick. One false step would have been dangerous on those narrow passes, but I felt no dizziness. I jumped a crevasse so deep it would have made me pause if I had been on land. I ventured out on a wobbling trunk, stretched across a chasm, without looking at my feet, because I had eyes only for the wild spectacles all about me. Monumental stones and natural towers and scarps, leaning on irregularly cut bases, seemed to defy the laws of equilibrium. From between their stony knees trees sprang like jets under heavy pressure, supporting others that supported them in turn.

Two hours after leaving the *Nautilus*, we had crossed the line of trees. A hundred feet above us rose the mountain summit, a dark silhouette against the brilliant irradiation. Petrified shrubs zigzagged here and there. From deep grottoes and holes in the rock I could sense dread things moving. My blood froze whenever I saw long antennae barring my path, or some pincer closing with a snap in the shade of some cavity. Millions of bright spots dotted the darkness. They were the eyes of giant crustacea crouched in their dens; of fearful octopi, their tentacles intertwining like nests of snakes.

We had now reached a plateau. Before us lay ruins—ruins that betrayed the hand of man, and not that of the Creator. Among vast heaps of stone there were discernible the shapes of palaces and temples, clothed now in blossoming zoophytes, covered not with ivy but with seaweed. What civilization was this that had been swallowed by some cataclysm? Where had Captain Nemo's whims brought me this time? I wanted to ask him; not being able to, I grabbed him by the arm. But he simply shook his head and pointed to the summit, as if to say: "Higher! Come higher!"

And so I followed, in a few minutes reaching the summit. Looking down in front of us, I could see that the drop was maybe twice that behind us—some sixteen hundred feet. My eyes ranged far over an immense area lit by violent flashes of light. As a matter of fact, this underwater mountain was a volcano!

Fifty feet below the summit, a large crater was spraying upward a rain of rocks and slag, and vomiting forth torrents of lava that streamed down the mountain. Of course there were no flames underwater, but the glow from the white-hot, incandescent lava lighted the lower plain like a vast torch. Nearby, ruined, flung down, lay a town—its roofs gone, its temples collapsed, its arches dislocated, yet all still displaying the solid proportions of a sort of Tuscan architecture! Over there was what remained of a great aqueduct; here, the foundation of an Acropolis and the floating form of a Parthenon. There lay the ruins of a pier, as if some antique port had vanished with its ships of commerce and triremes of war— and still farther out, the lines of sunken walls, of broad deserted avenues, all added up to a Pompeii beneath the waves.

Where was I? I had to know! I tried to ask, but Captain Nemo stopped me with a gesture. Picking up a bit of chalky rock, he walked up to a block of black basalt and traced out one word:

ATLANTIS

What lightning shot through my spirit! Atlantis, classed by many among the legends, but accepted by, among others, Plato, Pliny, Tertullian and Engel—there it was before my eyes, its own simple proof of its fate!

Plato tells us about an early attack on Athens by the Atlantides, people from an immense continent greater than Africa and Asia united, people whose hegemony extended even to Egypt. Centuries after they had failed to conquer Greece, a cataclysm overtook them, with floods and ground tremors, and in one night they fell into the sea, with only their highest summits—the Madeiras, Azores, Canaries—still above water.

Now I was standing on one of the mountains of that continent! I was walking where early man had walked!

While I was trying to fix every detail of this grandeur in my memory, Captain Nemo was leaning on a mossy pillar, motionless, as if petrified in a mute ecstasy. Was he dreaming of those generations long since disappeared? Was he asking them the secret of human destiny? At any rate we remained there for an entire hour, contemplating that plain stretched under the light of the lava. Then, standing up, Captain Nemo signaled me to follow him.

Descending the mountain quickly, we got on board the *Nautilus* just as the first rays of daylight whitened the surface of the sea.

I was so exhausted that I slept late that day, and went to bed again in the early evening. When I woke on the following morning, it was already eight a.m. Consulting the manometer, I could tell that we were on the surface, and indeed, I could hear steps on the platform. I went up the stairway and out, but—I saw not daylight but profound darkness!

Was I wrong about the time? Could it still be night? No, there was not a star in the sky. I did not know what to think, when a voice near me said, "Is that you, Monsieur Aronnax?"

"Captain," I answered, "where are we?"

"Underground, Professor."

"Underground! But we're floating!"

"The *Nautilus* always floats."

I confessed I didn't understand.

"Well, Professor, wait until our searchlight goes on."

Standing on the platform, waiting, I realized that it was so dark I had not seen even Captain Nemo. But looking to the zenith, I glimpsed a vague gleam, a kind of twilight covering a circular opening. Then the light went on, and its brightness dispelled the faint gleam.

The *Nautilus* was stationary, floating on a lake, imprisoned by a circle of walls about two miles in diameter. The tall walls, leaning toward each other, reached up to form a vaulted roof, like an immense funnel turned upside down. At the top, maybe fifteen hundred feet above us, was a round opening, through which I had seen the gleam of light, apparently daylight.

"Where are we?" I asked again.

"In the heart of an extinct volcano, Professor. Its interior was invaded by the sea after some great convulsion of the earth. That hole at the top is the crater. It supplies us with fresh air. You were sleeping when the *Nautilus* entered a natural canal—which opens about ten yards beneath the surface—and floated out on this lagoon. This is the *Nautilus'* harbor of refuge. Do you know of any other harbor that provides such perfect shelter?"

"You're perfectly safe here," I acknowledged. "But the *Nautilus* doesn't need a haven. So what good is this shelter?"

"The *Nautilus* needs electricity, and the wherewithal to make electricity—for that, as I once told you, I need sodium; hence, coal from which to get the sodium. And right here the sea covers entire forests, swallowed up during the geological periods. For me they now provide an inexhaustible mine of coal."

"Then here your sailors work as miners?"

"Precisely. Dressed in diving suits, pickaxe in hand, my men submerge and bring up the coal. When I burn the coal to make sodium, the smoke, escaping from the crater of the mountain, makes it look like an *active* volcano!"

"May I watch your crew at work?"

"Not this time. I'm eager to resume our submarine tour as soon as possible. I'm simply drawing on my reserve supplies. It will take the crew only a short time to load enough sodium for our trip."

THE FOLLOWING DAY, sailing a few fathoms below the surface of the Atlantic, we seemed to be steering clear of all land. Obviously, we would have to put aside for the time being our hopes of returning to European waters. For Captain Nemo continued to steer south. Where was he taking us? I couldn't even imagine.

For almost three weeks, the *Nautilus* traveled at a constant speed of a hundred leagues every twenty-four hours. Nothing unusual occurred during this period. The captain was hard at work and I rarely saw him. Sometimes I would find his books lying open in the library, especially books on natural history. My own work on the submarine mysteries I found covered with marginal notes, many of them contradicting my theories. But the captain was satisfied with correcting my book; he never discussed my ideas with me personally. Sometimes I heard the melancholy tones of the organ, but only at night.

We sailed whole days on the surface. The sea seemed abandoned. Once, however, we were pursued by a whaler who apparently thought we were a cetacean. But Captain Nemo, not wanting them to waste their time and effort, ended the chase by submerging.

Then, on March 13, we were engaged in taking soundings. We had then made about thirteen thousand leagues since our starting point in the Pacific. Our bearings gave us latitude 45° 37′ south, longitude 37° 53′ west. These were the same waters in which Lieutenant Parker of the United States frigate *Congress* had not been able to find the bottom with soundings of 7570 fathoms!

Captain Nemo planned to reach the sea floor at this point by traveling a long diagonal, his lateral fins set at an angle of forty-five degrees. He got up his maximum speed and the propeller's four blades beat the water with indescribable force. Under the great pressure the hull quivered like a sonorous chord, but we went down, down, and farther down.

Sitting in the salon, the captain and I watched the manometer needle move quickly. Soon we had dived below the lowest level at which most fish can survive. We saw only such creatures as the telescope fish, with its enormous eyes and armored malarmat, and a grenadier—this last at four thousand feet, under a pressure of a hundred and twenty atmospheres.

At seven thousand fathoms I could see black peaks rising from the depths below us! Those summits could belong to high mountains like the Himalayas or Mont Blanc! But, in spite of the pressure, the *Nautilus* descended farther. I could feel the steel plates trembling at their joints, I heard the bulkheads groan! The windows in the salon seemed to curve in.

Skirting the rocky peaks, whose bases were lost in the sea, I still saw some asteriads and other representatives of animal life.

"How do you explain life at these depths?" the captain asked me.

"There are vertical currents that produce enough movement to foster simple existence," I told him. "And the amount of oxygen dissolved in salt water actually increases with depth."

"You land scientists actually know that?" He was surprised.

Eventually, however, the *Nautilus* passed the limits of submarine life, just as a balloon can pass the limits of life in our atmosphere. We had reached a depth of 8535 fathoms, about 51,200 feet, and the hull was withstanding a pressure of twenty-four thousand pounds on each square inch of surface!

"What an experience!" I exclaimed to Captain Nemo. "To run over these regions where man has never visited! Look at those magnificent rocks, those uninhabited grottoes! What a pity that we cannot take away more than just the memory of it!"

"Would you like to take away a photograph?" the captain said.

Before I could express my surprise, a sailor brought a camera into the salon. Outside our panels, the waters were bright with electric light. In a few seconds we had a negative of extraordinary purity.

I still have the positive. It shows those primordial granite rocks never visited by the light of heaven; those deep grottoes with outlines so black, so sharp, they seem to have been painted by Flemish artists, and beyond these shapes and shades an undulating line of mountains! I only wish that I could describe it better.

"But now," Captain Nemo said, "we must go back up. We can't expose the *Nautilus* to such great pressures for too long a time. Hold on tight!"

Before I could understand the captain's command, I was flung down on the carpet. The screw had been disengaged at a signal from the captain, and the *Nautilus* shot up like a balloon released into the air. In four minutes we passed through four leagues of water! Emerging like a flying fish, the *Nautilus* leaped into the daylight, fell down again onto the Atlantic, and sent up great geysers to a prodigious height.

XIV. DISCOVERING THE SOUTH POLE

I HAD IMAGINED that when he reached the latitude of Cape Horn Captain Nemo would steer westward for the Pacific and so complete his world tour. But he did nothing of the kind. He headed always south. Where was he going? To the Pole? So far, every attempt to reach the South Pole had failed. And the season was well advanced. March in the Antarctic corresponds to September in the northern regions. I began to think that the Captain's temerity corroborated Ned's worst fear—that the captain might be insane.

The Canadian no longer spoke of his plans for escape, and he was less communicative. His long imprisonment was beginning to tell on him. When he saw the captain, his eyes burned with anger. I feared that someday he would be tempted to violence.

On March 14, he came to my cabin with Conseil. "How many crew do you think are on board the *Nautilus*, Professor?"

"I honestly don't know, Ned. But ten men ought to be enough, if you think only of operating the ship."

"What else should I be thinking of?"

I looked at him. It was easy to tell what he had on his mind. "The *Nautilus* is not just a ship that needs a crew," I said. "It is also a refuge for men who are exiles."

"But in any event," Conseil said, "the *Nautilus* can hold only a certain number of men. Could the professor estimate that number?"

"How, Conseil?"

"The professor knows the size of the ship, and hence the quantity of air it can hold. He knows also how much air each man uses, and he knows that the *Nautilus* must surface every twenty-four hours."

"But such calculations won't give us very useful answers."

"Try anyhow," Ned urged.

"Here is the calculation then," I said. "Each man consumes twenty-four hundred liters of oxygen in twenty-four hours. The *Nautilus* displaces fifteen hundred tons, and therefore it could contain one million, five hundred thousand liters of air. Divided by twenty-four hundred, that gives six hundred and twenty-five. Strictly speaking, then, the *Nautilus* could carry enough air for six hundred and twenty-five men for twenty-four hours."

"Six hundred and twenty-five!" Ned gasped.

"But remember, we have no way of knowing how many passengers and sailors are actually on board."

"Still too many, surely, for three men," Conseil murmured.

"My poor Ned," I said. "Patience! Patience!"

"Even better than patience," Conseil said, "is resignation!"

He had used the right word. The Canadian shook his head, ran his hand over his brow, and left the cabin.

"Will the professor permit me one observation?" Conseil said. "Poor Ned is nostalgic for everything he cannot have. And we owe it to him to try to understand him. He is not learned and cultured like the professor. He does not have the same love for the beauties of nature that the professor and his servant have. He would risk his life right now for just one night in a Canadian tavern!"

I knew that the routine on board was monotonously tame for Ned; but later that day something happened that reminded him of all the glories of his past life.

About eleven a.m. we were seated on the platform, studying a quiet sea, when Ned sighted a whale on the eastern horizon. Soon we could all see its black back rising and falling with the waves.

"If I were on a whaler now," Ned said, "this would be a great moment. Confound it, why am I confined to this steel tub!"

"Poor Ned," I said, "you never give up hope!"

"A whaler can't forget his trade, Professor. There's never a dull moment chasing a whale! Look! There's more than one of them, and they're coming closer! They know I can't go after them, they're tormenting me!" He stamped his foot. His hand trembled as if he held an imaginary harpoon. "There are ten! Twenty! An entire herd! And I can't do a thing! I'm tied hand and foot!"

"Ned," Conseil broke in, "why don't you ask the captain whether you can chase them?"

Before Conseil could finish his question, Ned had run to the hatch and gone below in search of Captain Nemo. A few minutes later they came out together on the platform. The captain watched the cetaceans playing on the waters about a mile away.

"Southern whales," he said, "enough to make the fortunes of a whole fleet of whalers."

"Captain," Ned asked, "may I go after them?"

"And why?" the captain demanded. "Just to kill them? We don't use whale oil on board the *Nautilus!*"

"But Captain, you let us go after the dugong!"

"Certainly. We needed the meat. But here it would be killing for killing's sake. I know that is a privilege reserved for mankind, but I do not approve of such murderous pastimes. The southern whale— like the Greenland whale of your home seas, Master Land—is a harmless creature. Hunting them down in quantities, the way you do, you are guilty of crimes against nature! Whalers are annihilating a whole class of useful animals. Leave the whales alone! They have enough natural enemies without your adding to their troubles!"

I felt that the captain was right, but Ned whistled "Yankee Doodle" through his teeth, and turned his back.

"I was right in saying they had enemies enough," the captain said. "Do you see those black points, about eight miles to leeward?"

"Yes," I said.

"Cachalots—sperm whales. They are cruel, terrible creatures. Man has good reason to exterminate *them*."

The Canadian turned around eagerly.

"Well, Captain," I said, "there's still time—on behalf of the whales!"

"It is useless to expose yourself, Professor. The *Nautilus* will disperse them. She is armed with a steel spur about as good as Master Land's harpoon, I imagine."

Ned didn't even bother to shrug his shoulders. Fight cetaceans with a spur attached to the bow! Whoever heard of such a thing?

"Just wait, Professor," the captain added. "We'll show you something new. We shall have no mercy on these ferocious beasts. They are nothing but mouth and teeth."

Mouth and teeth! What an excellent description of the cachalot! It is sometimes seventy-five feet long. Its enormous head occupies about one third of its body. Better armed and able to stay underwater longer than other whales, the cachalot is equipped with twenty-five pointed tusks, each about ten inches long. In the upper part of its enormous head it may carry six or eight hundred pounds of that precious oil called spermaceti.

As the formidable herd prepared to attack the whales, the *Nautilus* submerged. Conseil, Ned and I stationed ourselves at the salon windows and Captain Nemo went to the pilot's cage. Soon I felt the propeller turning more rapidly, and we shot ahead.

The battle between the cachalots and the whales was already in progress when we arrived. The cachalots at first showed no fear of this new monster joining the fight. But they were soon wary of its blows, for the *Nautilus* was a formidable harpoon brandished by

Captain Nemo. Hurled against a huge body, it passed through it, leaving behind two quivering halves of animal. Whenever one cachalot was cut in two, the *Nautilus* would then run at another, tacking to follow its prey, going back and forth, up and down, cutting and tearing in all directions.

This Homeric slaughter continued for an hour, until the cachalots suddenly joined forces, ten or twelve of them together trying to crush the *Nautilus* with their weight. We could see their huge mouths studded with tusks, the huge billows created by their beating tails; we could feel their bodies clinging to our ship like dogs worrying a wild boar in a copse. But the *Nautilus* carried them here and there, undaunted.

Finally, the mass broke up, the waves grew calmer, and I could tell that we were rising to the surface. The hatches opened and we hurried out on the platform. The sea, dyed red for miles, was strewn with mutilated, gigantic corpses, blue-backed and white-bellied. A few terrified cachalots were fleeing toward the horizon.

Captain Nemo joined us. "Well, Master Land?" he said.

"Well, Captain," Ned replied, "it was a spectacle certainly. But I'm not a butcher. I'm a hunter. This was butchery."

"It was a massacre of malevolent creatures. My *Nautilus* is not a butcher's knife!"

I was afraid they would fight it out, but luckily their attention was diverted by the sight of a whale that had not escaped the teeth of the cachalots. It was lying on its side, riddled with tusk bites, dead. Its open mouth let the water flow in and out, murmuring like waves on the shore. From its mutilated fin hung a young whale that it had not been able to save from the massacre.

Captain Nemo steered closer to the corpse. Two of his sailors leaped on its side. They drew from the whale's udders two or three barrels of milk! The captain offered me a cup, assuring me that it was not to be distinguished from cow's milk. I tasted it—it was still quite warm—and I agreed with him. Made later into butter and cheese, it proved to be a welcome addition to our usual fare as the *Nautilus*, remaining on the surface, kept steadily to its southerly course, following the fiftieth meridian.

ON MARCH 14 I SAW FLOATING ICE in latitude 55°, pieces of milky rubble, fifteen to thirty feet long, forming little reefs over which the sea unfurled and foamed. Toward the southern horizon there was a dazzling white streak across the heavens. English whalers have dubbed it "ice blink." No matter how thick the clouds may be, the ice blink will also always be there, announcing the presence of an ice pack or an ice field.

The farther south we moved, the bigger and more numerous the icebergs became. Some of them were streaked with green, as though veined with copper sulphate. Others looked like enormous amethysts, with the light behind them; others, colored by their limestone content, looked like masses of marble—quarries enough to build whole cities. Polar birds—puffins, petrels, damiers—nested on them by the thousands, deafening us with their cries.

Captain Nemo steered with consummate skill between these icy shapes, which were often two or three miles long and maybe two hundred feet high. Even when we reached 60° latitude, and there seemed to be no passes at all, he would still find a narrow pass and slip through it, knowing, of course, that it would close behind us.

On March 16, about eight a.m., we cut the Antarctic Circle at the fifty-fifth meridian. Our outside thermometer indicated twenty-seven to twenty-eight degrees Fahrenheit, or two or three degrees below zero Centigrade. But we were warmly clad with fur, thanks to the bear and the seal, and the interior of our ship was warmed by its electric heaters. Two months earlier we would have had continuous daylight in these latitudes. But now we had nights three or four hours long. And soon there would be continuous night, six months of darkness in these circumpolar regions.

During the day of March 16 a vast ice field absolutely blocked our passage. The captain flung his *Nautilus* against the brittle mass, splitting it with frightful crackings. Thrown high in the air, ice fell like hail all about us. Next moment, carried by its own momentum, the *Nautilus* landed on top of the ice, crushing part of the field with its weight. In this way, our boat made its own channel.

Then storms hit us, bringing with them thick fogs through which we could see nothing. The wind blew sharply, the snow packed itself down so tight we had to go out and break it with pickaxes, and the *Nautilus* became covered with ice. A vessel with rigging would never have made it; the tackle would have become frozen solid.

And now the compass needle would point in all directions as we got nearer to the south magnetic pole, not to be confused with the South Pole itself. We had to take several readings on compasses placed in different parts of the ship and then strike a mean!

On March 17, after many fruitless assaults against the ice, the *Nautilus* seemed locked in. Our position was longitude 51° 30′, latitude 67° 39′. We had advanced deep into the Antarctic! What lay ahead was a huge barrier, formed by icebergs cemented together!

"The great ice shelf!" Ned said with awe.

I knew that to the Canadian, and to other mariners who had come before us, this looked like a hopeless obstacle. When the sun appeared at midday, we could see nothing of the *liquid* surface of the sea. Beyond the *Nautilus'* spur lay a frozen plain. Here and there we could see sharp peaks, ice needles rising some two hundred feet; farther on, a row of steep gray cliffs reflected the sunlight like tall, tilted mirrors half hidden by fogs. Over this desolate face of nature a stark silence reigned, occasionally broken by puffins and petrels flapping their wings. Everything was frozen, even the sounds.

Usually, when we could go no farther, we could always go back. But here every pass had closed behind us. About two p.m., when Captain Nemo and I were on the platform, fresh ice began to form around our hull.

"Looks as if we're caught, Captain," I said.

"Professor, do you really think the *Nautilus* can't get free?" he asked.

"Captain, the season is too far advanced for you to count on being able to break up the ice."

"You see nothing but difficulties, Professor. I tell you, the *Nautilus* will not only free herself, she will go farther south!"

"Farther south?"

"She shall go to the Pole."

"To the Pole!" I couldn't conceal my incredulity.

"To the Antarctic Pole, that unknown point where no man has ever yet set foot. We shall discover it together, Professor!"

"I can believe you, Captain," I said with irony. "Let's go! There are no obstacles for us! Smash that ice shelf! Blow it up! If it still resists, let the *Nautilus* fly over it!"

"Not over it," Captain Nemo said quietly. "*Under* it."

"Under it!" Suddenly I understood how the peculiar talents of the *Nautilus* were going to serve us in this superhuman enterprise!

"We begin to understand each other." The captain smiled. "You begin to see the possibility—I should say, the success—of this attempt. If a continent lies before the South Pole, then we must stop at the continent. But if, on the contrary, the South Pole, like the North Pole, is washed by the open sea, we'll go right there!"

"Yes." I was carried away by his reasoning. "If the surface is frozen, at least the lower depths are still liquid, according to that law of nature which places the maximum density of the ocean one degree higher than freezing point."

"Yes, and although for every foot of iceberg above the sea there are three below it, those three-hundred-foot icebergs over there are not more than nine hundred feet below the surface. And what are nine hundred feet for the *Nautilus?*"

"Nothing at all."

The captain gave certain orders to the lieutenant, who seemed not a bit surprised. But he could never have been as impassive as Conseil, who simply said, when I told him about our destination, "Whatever pleases monsieur." Ned, on the other hand, went to his cabin to prevent himself, as he said, "from blowing up."

Preparations were under way. The powerful pumps were forcing extra supplies of air into the reservoirs, storing it at high pressure. About four p.m. twelve men, armed with pickaxes, chopped away the ice around the *Nautilus*. Then we all went below, and the *Nautilus* submerged.

About nine hundred feet down, just as Captain Nemo had predicted, we were sailing *beneath* the ice shelf! We were aiming directly at the Pole along the fifty-second meridian and still had twenty-two and a half degrees of latitude to go, or about five hundred leagues. The *Nautilus* was averaging twenty-six knots. If we maintained that, we would reach the Pole in forty hours.

The novelty of the situation kept Conseil and myself at the salon windows until two a.m. The sea was lit by our searchlight, but it was deserted. Fish do not linger in these imprisoned waters.

We were back at our windows at five a.m., March 18. From the electric log I could see that our speed had been slackened. We were rising, but slowly. My heart beat fast. Would we be able to surface? No! I could feel a collision! We had struck the bottom of the ice shelf three thousand feet below the surface. This meant that there were four thousand feet of ice shelf above us, one thousand feet of it rising above the surface! Here, then, the ice shelf was even higher than it had been at its edges. Not very reassuring.

Several times that day the *Nautilus* tried again, and each time it struck the solid mass that lay like a ceiling over us. By nightfall the ice had gradually diminished to fifteen hundred or twelve hundred feet in thickness, but that was still a quite impenetrable wall between us and the surface!

My sleep was painful that night. Hope and fear possessed me by turns. Several times I got up. The *Nautilus* continued to grope.

About three a.m., I noticed that our depth was only a hundred and fifty feet! The shelf was gradually thinning! I never took my eyes off the manometer. We were still ascending diagonally.

At last, at six a.m. on March 19, Captain Nemo opened the salon door. "The open sea!" he said.

I RUSHED OUT ON THE PLATFORM. Yes! Except for a few scattered icebergs, a long stretch of sea! The thermometer read three degrees above zero Centigrade, or thirty-seven degrees Fahrenheit. This was like spring, compared to what we had known beyond the ice shelf, whose long mass I could see on the horizon behind us.

"Are we at the Pole?" I asked with a beating heart.

"I can't tell yet," the captain answered. "I'll take our bearings at noon."

"Will the sun get through this fog?" I looked at the leaden sky.

"No matter how little it shows, it will suffice."

About ten miles to the south, or what seemed to be the south, a solitary island rose to a height of about six hundred and fifty feet. We circled it carefully. Its circumference measured about five miles. A narrow channel separated it from a considerable stretch of mainland, perhaps a continent.

For fear of running aground, the *Nautilus* stopped about three cable lengths from a beach on this mainland, above which rose a superb accumulation of rocks. The captain, two sailors carrying instruments, Conseil and I got into the dinghy. We had not seen Ned. Doubtless the harpooner did not wish to acknowledge the existence of the South Pole. It was ten a.m. Soon we neared the shore. Conseil was about to leap on land, but I held him back. "Captain Nemo, the honor of first setting foot on this land belongs to you!"

"I agree, Professor," he answered, "and if I don't hesitate to tread on the South Pole, it's because up to now no human being has left his mark there."

Vibrant with emotion, he jumped on land. Then he leaped on a rock, stepping out on a little promontory. With his arms crossed, mute and motionless, and with an eager scan, he seemed to be taking possession of this southern territory. After five minutes, he turned toward us. "Whenever you say, Professor."

I landed, followed by Conseil, leaving the two sailors in the boat. The earth was composed of a reddish volcanic rock, something like crushed brick. Vegetation on this desolate land seemed limited. I saw some lichens clinging to the rocks, some microscopic plants, and some purple fucus which the waves threw up on the shore. In the water near the shore I saw some zoophytes—shrublike corals that, according to the English explorer Ross, can live in Antarctic seas as far down as three thousand feet. The coast was strewn with mollusks, mussels and limpets.

But life most abounded in the air. Thousands of birds were flying, fluttering, deafening us with their cries. Others crowded the rocks and stared at us, all without fear. There were auks and albatrosses, and I saw a whole series of petrels, some white with brown-bordered wings. Half a mile on, the soil was riddled with penguins' nests. Captain Nemo had his men hunt down some of these birds, for their flesh is good food. They were big as geese, uttering cries like the braying of an ass.

The fog lingered, and at eleven the sun still had not shown itself. This made me uneasy. Without the sun no observations were possible. How could we know whether we had discovered the South Pole? The captain kept staring at the sky. He was vexed and impatient, but he could not command the sun. When noon came, it was sunless. The mist turned into snow. "Tomorrow, then," the captain said quietly, and we returned to the *Nautilus*.

But the snowy tempest lasted all the following day. The *Nautilus* spent the time skirting the coast in the half-light. If we could not shoot the sun the next day, it would be calamitous. Next day would be March 21, the equinox: then the sun would drop below the horizon for six months, the long polar night would begin!

Nobody was more aware of the situation than Captain Nemo himself. However, he explained to me that, if the sun did show itself the following day, his bearings would be very easy to take.

"Since tomorrow is the equinox," he explained, "I shall take my chronometer and if, at noon, the disk of the sun—allowing for refraction, of course—is precisely cut by the northern horizon, I shall know quite simply that I am at the South Pole."

After breakfast on March 21, the *Nautilus* was standing a good league off from the coast, over which rose a sharp peak about fifteen hundred feet tall.

"The weather is letting up a little," the captain said. "Let's go ashore and find an observation post."

I wanted Ned to come along on this historic day, but his ill mood was getting worse by the day and he refused. So the small boat took over Captain Nemo, Conseil and myself, together with a chronometer, a telescope and a barometer.

We landed at nine a.m. The sky was brightening, the clouds were flying away, the fog was lifting from the water. Captain Nemo headed for the peak near the coast. It was a difficult climb over sharp lava and pumice stones, and it took us two hours to reach the summit. Below and in front of us were fields of dazzling whiteness, together with a chaotic accumulation of rocks and ice blocks; and above us was a sky of pale azure. To the north the sun was a ball of fire, already cut by the horizon. Behind us lay the *Nautilus*, like a cetacean asleep on the surface of the sea.

At the top of the peak, Captain Nemo calculated its altitude with his barometer, for he would have to consider that when determining our position.

At eleven forty-five a.m., the sun, visible now only by refraction, was shedding its last rays over this deserted continent, over seas that men had never before crossed. The captain, using a reticulated telescope to correct the refraction, watched it sinking below the horizon by degrees, following a long diagonal. I held the chronometer. My heart was beating hard.

"Twelve!" I cried out.

"The South Pole," the captain replied in a grave voice. He handed me the reticulated glass, which showed the orb cut in equal halves by the horizon.

I watched the last rays hitting the peak, the shadows mounting gradually up the slope.

The captain suddenly put his hand on my shoulder and said, "Professor, in 1600, the Dutchman Gheritk reached the sixty-fourth parallel. In 1774, the illustrious Cook attained latitude 71° 15′ south. In 1825 a simple English seal fisherman, Weddell, actually reached latitude 74° 15′ south. Finally, in 1842, the Englishman James Ross discovered Victoria Land, later taking his bearings in 78° 4′, the highest latitude ever reached before today.

"And now, I, Captain Nemo, on March twenty-first, 1868, have reached 90°—the South Pole! And I take possession of this part of the globe equal to one sixth of the known continents!"

"In whose name, Captain?"

"In my name, Professor."

Then he unfurled a black banner, bearing the letter N embroidered in gold. Turning toward the sun, whose last rays were just touching the horizon of the sea, he cried:

"Adieu, sun! Sleep beneath this open sea, and let a night six months long extend its shadows over my new domains!"

THE STARS WERE SHINING with wondrous intensity in the polar night as we got ready to leave the South Pole at six a.m., March 22. At the zenith glittered the Southern Cross. The thermometer read twelve degrees below zero Centigrade, and fresh ice was forming in the open sea.

We headed quickly north. Toward noon, the *Nautilus* submerged, and by evening we were sailing beneath the great ice shelf. Restless, I lay awake. It was late before I could sleep. At three o'clock the next morning, March 23, I was aroused by a violent shock. I sat up and listened in the dark. Then I was flung into the center of the room. Apparently the *Nautilus* had struck and then rebounded.

I felt my way through the passage and into the lighted salon. The furniture was upset. Fortunately the glass cases were firmly set in place, but pictures on the starboard side were *lying* on the wall, while pictures on the port side were hanging a foot away from their wall! The *Nautilus* was over on its starboard side, motionless. I heard a babble of voices, and Ned and Conseil came in.

"What's wrong?" I asked.

"We came to ask the professor," Conseil said.

"Confound it!" the Canadian exclaimed. "I know what's wrong! The *Nautilus* has struck! And judging from the way she lies, I don't think she'll right herself the way she did in the Torres Strait!"

I consulted the manometer. We were a hundred and eighty fathoms down! "What can that mean?" I exclaimed.

At that moment Captain Nemo entered the salon. His face, usually impassive, showed signs of anxiety. He went from the compass to the manometer to the planisphere. When at last he turned toward me, I spoke that phrase he had used in the Torres Strait: "An incident?"

"No, Professor, this time it's an accident."

"Serious?"

"Maybe. We are stranded."

"How has it happened?"

"Not by our ignorance, but by a whim of nature. An enormous block of ice, a whole mountain, has turned over. When an iceberg is undermined by warmer water, or by repeated shocks, its center of gravity shifts and it may capsize. This is what has happened: one of these falling blocks has hit the *Nautilus* and slid under our hull. It has floated upward, lifting us with it. We are lying on our side on this submerged slab of ice!"

"Can't we empty our tanks, regain our equilibrium, and rise off the block?"

"Professor, you can hear the pumps working. Look at the manometer—we're rising. But the slab of ice is rising too! Until it stops moving, we can't change our position."

Yes, the *Nautilus* still lay to starboard. Surely it would right itself when the block stopped rising? But suppose the block hit the underside of the great ice shelf? We would be crushed between the two masses of ice! Captain Nemo never took his eyes off the manometer. Since the fall of the iceberg the *Nautilus* had risen about a hundred and fifty feet, but it still lay over at an angle. Suddenly we could feel a slight movement of our hull. Things hanging in the salon began to return to their usual position. We watched, we felt the straightening. At last the floor seemed almost horizontal. "She's righted!"

"Yes." And Captain Nemo made for the door.

"But are we floating?" I asked.

"Of course. As we empty our tanks, we rise." He went out.

The salon panels opened and, since the searchlight was on, we could see all around. Yes, we were now suspended in the water. But there was a wall of ice on either side of us, not more than thirty feet away. Above us—the ice shelf stretched like an immense ceiling. Below us—there the overturned block had apparently slid into place at the base of the sidewalls. The *Nautilus* was imprisoned in a veritable tunnel of ice, filled with quiet water!

"This is the end," Ned murmured.

"No," I told him, "it should be easy to get out of the tunnel, either by going ahead or by backing up."

The overhead light in the salon went out, but still the room was splendidly illuminated by the reflection of the searchlight on the blocks of ice! Every ridge, every facet reflected a different hue, depending on the nature of the veins running through the ice—a dazzling collection of sapphires, emeralds, opals and diamonds.

"Isn't that a wonderful sight, Ned?" I asked.

"Yes, confound it! And I am angry at being forced to admit it! No one has ever seen anything like it. And it may turn out to be a very expensive view! I think we're looking at things that God never intended man to see!"

Suddenly Conseil cried out, and clapped his hands over his face. "I'm blinded!"

Indeed, I too could not stand the fire which seemed to consume the glass itself. The *Nautilus* had put on full speed. The luster of the ice walls had been transformed into flashes of dazzling lightning. Even though I closed my eyes tight, I continued to see bright concentric glimmerings.

When I could control my vision and look again at the clock, I saw that it was five a.m. At that moment we felt a collision at the bow. The *Nautilus* went into reverse.

"We're backing up?" Conseil wondered.

"Yes," I said. "I guess there's no way out at this end of the tunnel, so we'll go out the southern end."

I hoped I sounded more convinced than I really was. For a while I walked back and forth. My companions were quiet. Then I flung myself on a divan, picked up a book, and went through the motions of reading it. Later Conseil came over. "Does monsieur like that book?"

"Very good, Conseil. Yes, it's a good book."

"I'm glad to hear that. The professor is reading his own book."

"My book? This is . . . ?" Yes, I was holding in my hands my book on the great ocean depths. I had never even suspected it. Snapping it shut, I started walking up and down again. Ned and Conseil got up to go. "No, please stay. Let's stay together until we get out of this mess!"

"As monsieur wishes," Conseil answered.

During the next several hours I looked frequently at the instruments hanging from the bulkhead. The manometer showed that we were now sailing at a constant depth of nine hundred feet. The compass still pointed south. The log indicated a steady speed of twenty knots—fast for such a narrow passageway. But Captain Nemo knew that minutes were worth ages to us right now.

At eight twenty-five a.m. there was a second collision, this time at the stern. I'm sure I turned pale. I took Conseil's hand. Then the captain came into the salon.

"The southern end is blocked too?" I asked.

"Yes, Professor. The iceberg has shifted and closed every exit. We are trapped."

The Canadian slapped a table with his powerful hand. Conseil was quiet. I watched the captain. He had resumed his usual impassive manner. "Gentlemen," he said calmly, crossing his arms, "in our situation there are two ways to die. The first is to be crushed to death. The second is to die of asphyxiation. I rule out the chance of starving to death. Our food supply could actually outlast us. So let us calculate our chances."

"As for suffocating, Captain," I said, "what do we have to worry about? Our reserve tanks are full."

"Yes, but we have been underwater now for twenty hours. Tomorrow night we shall have to start using our reserves. In four days our reserves will be almost completely exhausted."

"Can we get out of here in that time?"

"We'll try, of course. We'll try to cut our way out. I'll run the *Nautilus* aground on the lower bank. We'll take soundings. My men will attack the ice on the side where we meet least resistance."

Decided on a course of action, he left the salon. Soon the *Nautilus* began to sink, resting finally a thousand feet down where the lower bank of ice had settled!

"Well"—I turned to my companions—"I guess we're in trouble this time. It's going to take a lot of courage and strength . . ."

"Professor," the Canadian said, "recently I have been boring you with my complaints. But you know I'm ready to do anything . . ."

"Of course, Ned, I never doubted it." We shook hands.

"And I'm as handy with a pickaxe as I am with a harpoon. If the captain needs me, I'm ready."

"He won't refuse your help. Come on, Ned." I led him to the room where some of the crew were putting on their diving suits. His offer accepted, Ned was soon encased in his underwater costume. Returning to the salon, Conseil and I watched through the window as twelve men set foot out on the ice.

Captain Nemo was commanding the operation in person. First the men sank long sounding lines into the sidewalls. After reaching fifteen yards they gave up. It was pointless to attack the ceiling, since we knew that the iceberg was at least thirteen hundred feet high at this point. (We had descended a thousand feet, and that meant there were at least three hundred feet of iceberg above the water.) Accordingly Captain Nemo sounded the lower surface. It turned out to be ten yards thick! Thirty feet down to water we could navigate!

It was necessary, then, to cut in the lower bank a hole equal in size and shape to the outline of the *Nautilus*. If we extended this hole down ten yards, we could then escape through it and get under the ice field. Roughly, this meant we had to detach about sixty-five hundred cubic yards of ice!

Instead of digging around the ship, which would have involved great difficulties, the captain decided to cut the hole about twenty-five feet away from our port quarter. The men attacked the ice with drills until they had outlined a long cigar shape. Then they used pickaxes to cut out rough blocks. Since a mass of ice is lighter than a mass of water of equal volume, we now witnessed this curious phenomenon: as the men detached each block of ice it floated to the roof of the tunnel! As a result, then, the roof was getting thicker as the base was getting thinner.

After two hours, Ned and his companions came in exhausted. Conseil and I joined the second shift.

The water seemed fiercely cold, but I warmed up as soon as I had handled the pickaxe for a few minutes. When I reentered the ship, two hours later, I could sense immediately the difference between the good air I had been breathing from the Rouquayrol apparatus and the foul air of the *Nautilus*, already charged with carbon dioxide.

After twelve hours of work, we had detached a layer of ice only one yard thick—only six hundred and fifty cubic yards. At that rate, it would take us another five nights and four days to complete the job. Our air supplies would never last that long. "Without taking into account," Ned added, "that even if we get out of this tunnel, we'll still be trapped under the ice shelf."

During the night a second layer, also a yard thick, had been floated out, and in the morning of March 24 I stepped down into a trench six feet deep. But as I moved around the slushy mass at the bottom, I noticed that the sidewalls of the tunnel were closer. The water farthest from the trench, not warmed by the men's work, was freezing. This new ice could close in and crush the hull of the *Nautilus* like glass! I didn't mention this new threat to Ned or Conseil, but as soon as I had a chance I told Captain Nemo.

"I know." He surprised me again with his calmness. "All I can suggest is that we work faster, faster than the water freezes."

Toward evening the trench was one yard deeper. When I went back on board, I was nearly asphyxiated by the carbon dioxide that filled the ship.

The next day, March 25, I resumed work by attacking the fifth yard. Looking up, again I could see that the sidewalls and the ceiling had thickened considerably—they were going to meet before the *Nautilus* was able to disengage itself! Back in the salon, I spoke of this to Captain Nemo.

"Professor," he replied, "either we think of a remedy, or we'll be sealed up as if by cement."

I had no remedy. "How long will our air tanks last?"

"The day after tomorrow, they will be quite empty." Suddenly an idea seemed to hit Captain Nemo. "Boiling water!" he muttered. "Why can't we use streams of boiling water to stop the freezing?"

"Why not!" I said resolutely.

The outside thermometer read nineteen degrees Fahrenheit. Seawater begins to freeze when it gets below twenty-nine degrees Fahrenheit. Captain Nemo led me back to the galleys, where he put the cooks to work on the distilling machines used to process sea-water for drinking. All available electric energy from the batteries was thrown into the coils bathed by the water. Soon the crew were injecting boiling water into the sea outside! Five hours later, the thermometer read twenty-five degrees Fahrenheit, and during the night the temperature of the water around us actually rose to thirty degrees Fahrenheit. The congelation of the surrounding water had been halted!

By the morning of March 26 we had detached six yards of ice; we had only four more to clear away. But that was still forty-eight hours' work, and the little air that remained in our tanks was kept solely for the workers outside; there was not a breath for the men on board. An unbearable weight oppressed me. I yawned so that I almost dislocated my jaws. My lungs panted as they inhaled the burning gas around me, which became more and more rarefied. I was on the verge of unconsciousness. Although he was suffering just as much, Conseil took my hand and encouraged me. "Monsieur must believe me," he said. "I would be willing to stop breathing, if it would help the professor. . . ."

I believed him. Tears came into my eyes.

With what haste, what joy we got into our underwater suits, to get that first whiff from the Rouquayrol apparatus! Flinging that pickaxe at the frozen ice made our arms ache; the skin was torn off our hands. But what did it matter, so long as we breathed!

That day we worked with unusual vigor. Only two yards to go! But by nightfall the air tanks were almost empty. By midnight I had a terrible headache; I was dizzy, nauseated. Some of the crew were breathing with a frightful rattling sound.

Realizing that the work was going too slowly, Captain Nemo decided to try to crush the ice that still separated us from the sea below. He gave orders to lighten the vessel, and so it was raised from the ice by a change in its specific gravity. When it was float-ing, the crew towed it slowly until it was just above the cigar-shaped trench cut deep in the ice. Filling the reservoirs with water, the captain settled the *Nautilus* into the hole. Then all the crew came aboard.

The *Nautilus* was resting on ice not more than a yard thick and perforated in thousands of places by the sounding leads. The valves were opened, and a hundred cubic yards of water were admitted into the tanks. We waited, listening, forgetting our pain, for our lives depended on this last maneuver. In spite of the buzzing in my head, I could hear a humming sound under the hull! Then, the ice gave way with a strange noise, like the tearing of paper, and the *Nautilus* dropped!

"We made it, monsieur!" Conseil murmured.

Speechless, I could only shake his hand. All at once, carried away by its terrific overload, the *Nautilus* sank like a cannonball in a vacuum. Then all the electric power was applied to the pumps, which soon began to force water out of the tanks. After a few minutes the manometer indicated a slow ascension! Going at full speed, the propeller made the iron hull tremble to its very bolts.

Yes, we were heading north, but if we could not come out from under the ice shelf, could not reach the open air soon, we would still all suffocate. Half stretched out on a divan in the library, I could neither see nor hear. I was conscious of death coming over me. Suddenly I revived. I was breathing oxygen! Had we surfaced? No. Ned and Conseil had found a small amount of compressed air in one of the Rouquayrol apparatuses.

I tried to push the thing away, to say we must share this remaining air, but they held my hands down. For some moments I breathed freely.

Then I found I had the strength to look at the clock. It was eleven a.m. The *Nautilus* was tearing through the water at forty knots. And now I could see the manometer. We were not more than twenty feet from the surface! A mere plate of ice separated us from fresh air! Could we break through it? Maybe. In any event, the *Nautilus* was going to try.

The stern was dropping, the bow was rising. The *Nautilus* was about to attack the ice field like a battering ram. At last, dashing full speed ahead, the ship shot through the ice, came out on top of it, and then crumpled it with its weight.

The hatches were opened and fresh air flooded into the *Nautilus*.

I CAN'T IMAGINE how I got out onto the platform. But I was there with my friends, and all three of us were getting drunk on fresh oxygen! The first words I spoke, when revived, were words of thanks, for Ned and Conseil had saved my life during the last hours of our ordeal.

"Please, Professor," Ned said. "It was just a question of basic arithmetic! You are more valuable to the world than we are!"

"No one is superior to a generous and good person like yourself, Ned. And you, too, my brave Conseil, you suffered much on my behalf! I am permanently indebted to you both; I feel bound to you forever."

"And I'll surely take advantage of that!" Ned exclaimed.

"How do you mean that?" Conseil asked.

"I mean that when I leave this confounded ship, I'll take you with me!"

"Yes," said Conseil suddenly, "but are we headed in the right direction?"

"We must be," I said. "We're heading toward the sun, and here, the sun is north."

"But are we heading toward the deserted Pacific or the frequented Atlantic?" Ned asked.

I could not say; but Ned's answer came on March 31, when we were off Cape Horn. I could then see from the planisphere, to my great satisfaction, that we were continuing north by way of the Atlantic. The *Nautilus* followed the long windings of the South American coast. On April 3 we crossed the Tropic of Capricorn. It seemed that Captain Nemo—much to Ned's annoyance—did not like the inhabited coasts of Brazil, because we passed them at a dizzy speed, and when we sighted the easternmost point of South America, Saõ Roque Cape, the *Nautilus* sought the greatest depths of the submarine valley that runs between this cape and Sierra Leone on the African coast.

Then, after crossing the equator, we surfaced on April 11 near the mouth of the Amazon, a vast estuary whose flow of fresh water is so great that it sweetens the seawater for miles around. Twenty miles to the west lay French Guiana, where we could easily have taken refuge. But, although the *Nautilus* never left the surface for two days, a stiff breeze was blowing, whipping up waves too wild for a small boat to face.

I meanwhile passed the time pleasantly engrossed in my studies. On April 11 and 12, the *Nautilus* set dragnets, and these brought in a marvelous haul of fish and reptiles. I noticed several species of fish that I had not yet had an opportunity to study, including "pteromyzons-pricka," a kind of eel with a green head, violet fins, and the iris of the eye circled with gold. There were also curassavians with brilliant gold spots; numbers of clear violet ca-priscus; sardines ten inches long, resplendently silver; and orange-colored giltheads with long tongues. In particular, I must mention a fish that Conseil will remember for a long time to come.

One of our nets had pulled in a flat disk-shaped ray which weighed about forty pounds. It was red on the bottom, white on top, with large spots of dark blue encircled with black, and with very glossy skin. Stretched out on the platform, it struggled to throw itself back into the sea. But Conseil rushed to prevent it, and before I could warn him he seized it with both hands. He fell back on the platform, half paralyzed, crying, "Monsieur! Help me!"

Ned and I massaged him until his limbs relaxed, and when he had regained his senses that perpetual classifier murmured, "Cartilaginous class, order of chondropterygians, selachian suborder, family of rays, genus of crampfish . . ."

"Yes, my friend," I said, "that was a crampfish!"

He had attacked the most dangerous kind, the cumana. So great is the electric power of this bizarre animal that he can shock a fish several yards away! "I'll get my revenge," Conseil muttered. "I'll eat him." And although the creature was tough as leather, Conseil did eat some of him.

Continuing its voyage, the *Nautilus* steered clear of the American coast for several days. Evidently it did not want to enter the Gulf of Mexico or the Caribbean—probably there were too many steamers in these regions for its comfort. On April 16 we sighted Martinique and Guadeloupe about thirty miles away.

Ned was disheartened. Recently he had been counting on escaping in the Gulf. We had been prisoners on the *Nautilus* for six months. As the Canadian said, there was no reason to believe that our journey would ever come to an end. And so he proposed to me that we put this categorical question to the captain: *Do you intend to keep us prisoners indefinitely?*

This proposal seemed unwise to me. I felt that we could expect no mercy from the captain, that we had to rely on ourselves for help. Besides, for some time now the captain had been more withdrawn, less sociable. He seemed to shun me. What had caused this change in attitude? Had our presence on board become too great an inconvenience to him? That still was no reason to suppose that he would give us our liberty!

I asked Ned to let me reflect on his plan. After all, if it did not work, it could revive the captain's suspicions and hamper other possible projects. I must add that I certainly could not give our physical condition as a reason for wanting our freedom. With the exception of that ordeal under the ice shelf, we had probably never known better health. For a Captain Nemo, such a life was all too understandable. But, as Ned pointed out, *we* had not severed all ties with humanity. And for my part, I did not want *my* studies to die with *me*. I now had it within my power to write the truly definitive book about the sea, and I wanted this book, sooner or later, to see daylight.

And here again, in these West Indies waters, what interesting data I was still entering in my notebooks! On April 20 we were cruising at a depth of about five thousand feet off the Bahamas. Outside the panels, Ned, Conseil and I could see high submarine cliffs, carpeted with huge seaweeds, giant laminariae and fuci, truly a bower of hydrophytes worthy of a Titan world.

"These colossal plants would form the perfect food for giant squid," I said, "and I would not be astonished to see some of those monsters."

"Do you mean those giant cephalopods that can drag ships

down into the abyss?" said Conseil. "I'd like to come face-to-face with one. They're known as krakens, I think."

"You'll never get me to believe in such creatures," said Ned.

"Why not?" Conseil asked. "Didn't we believe in the professor's giant narwhal?"

"And we were wrong, Conseil."

"Well, I myself," Conseil said with the most serious air imaginable, "can remember seeing a large ship dragged under the water in the arms of such a cephalopod."

"And do you mind telling me where?" the Canadian demanded.

"At Saint-Malo," Conseil replied imperturbably.

"In the harbor, I suppose?"

"No, inside a church. Mind you, it was a painting that represented the squid in question."

"That's a good one." Ned laughed. "Professor, he put one over on me."

"Conseil is quite right," I said. "I have heard about that painting. But the story it portrays is taken from a legend, and you know what to think of legends when it comes to natural history. Nevertheless, there are so many legends about such monsters that there must have been something real that gave rise to them. We cannot deny that there are species of octopus and cuttlefish that grow to great size. The most astonishing event verifying the existence of these creatures happened just recently, in 1861."

"What was that?" Ned asked.

"Well, northeast of Tenerife in just about the latitude that we're in now, the crew of the dispatch boat *Alecton* saw a huge squid. Captain Bouguer attacked the animal with harpoons and guns, but the harpoons and bullets passed right through the soft flesh as though it were jelly. Finally the crew managed to pass a slipknot around the body of the mollusk. But when they tried to haul the monster aboard, it was so heavy that the rope just tightened and cut off the tail. Deprived of that ornament, the creature disappeared under the waves. As a result of this encounter, it was suggested that this type of cephalopod be called 'Bouguer's squid.'"

"How long was it?" Ned asked.

"It must have been about twenty feet long," Conseil said.

"Exactly," I replied.

"And wasn't its head crowned with eight tentacles that beat the water like a nest of serpents?" Conseil went on.

"Precisely."

"And wasn't its mouth like a parakeet's beak, but huge?"

"Yes, Conseil," I said.

"Well, with monsieur's permission," he said quietly, "this is either Bouguer's squid or one of his brothers."

I looked toward Conseil, and could not prevent myself from shrinking back in dismay. Before my eyes a terrible squid of colossal dimensions, about twenty-five feet long, was moving toward the *Nautilus*. Regarding us with enormous blue-green eyes, it fastened one of its eight arms onto the glass window by means of the suckers on the inside of the tentacle. Its horny beak opened and its tongue, also horny, came out quivering from between these shears. Its body was a spindle-shaped mass of flesh that must have weighed between forty-five and fifty-five thousand pounds! Its color varied constantly, according to the mood of the animal, ranging from a livid gray to a red-brown.

Chance alone had brought me into the presence of this freak of nature, which has three hearts, and I did not want to lose the opportunity to study it in the safety of the *Nautilus*. I overcame my revulsion and took out a pencil and began to draw.

"Maybe this is the same one that got away from the *Alecton*," Conseil said.

"No, this one hasn't lost his tail," Ned said.

"That wouldn't matter," I said. "The arms and tails of these creatures can re-form by a special process called redintegration."

"So, if this isn't Bouguer's squid, then he's probably one of those over there!" Ned said.

Indeed, other tremendous squid were approaching the starboard window. I counted seven! They had formed a procession around the *Nautilus*, and I could hear the sound of their beaks grating on the steel hull. Then all of a sudden the *Nautilus* stopped! There was a shock which made it tremble in every member.

"Have we struck? Are we aground?" I asked.

"We're still floating," Ned answered.

The *Nautilus* was floating, no doubt, but not moving. A minute passed. Captain Nemo, followed by his lieutenant, entered the salon. Without speaking, he went to the window, looked at the squid and said a few words to his lieutenant, who then left. Soon the panels were closed.

"A curious collection of squid," I said to the captain casually.

"Yes, *monsieur le naturaliste*," he answered. "And we are going to take them on—hand to hand."

"Hand to hand?"

"Yes. The propeller has been stopped. One of these squid got his beak caught in the blades. That's why we can't move. I'm going to surface and massacre the vermin."

"A difficult enterprise."

"Yes. Their soft flesh does not offer enough resistance to make our bullets explode. We'll have to use hatchets."

"And a harpoon, Captain," Ned said, "if you'll accept my help."

"Accepted, Master Land."

"We'll all go," I said.

At the central staircase, a dozen men, armed with axes, were set for the attack. Conseil and I each took an axe, and Ned seized a harpoon. The *Nautilus* had surfaced. One of the sailors, at the top of the ladder, was unbolting the hatch. Hardly were the bolts loose when the hatch flew open, evidently pulled up by the suckers on a squid's arm. Immediately one arm slid like a serpent down the staircase, while several others were moving about above us. Captain Nemo, with one blow of his axe, cut through this tentacle, and it fell squirming down the ladder.

Just as we were crowding up the ladder, two other arms, lashing the air, descended on the sailor just ahead of Captain Nemo and pulled him up. Captain Nemo rushed out on the platform. We were right behind.

What a scene! The unfortunate sailor, held by the tentacle, was being waved about in the air. He gasped, and cried, "Help! Help!"

These words, spoken in French, stupefied me! So I had a compatriot on board, perhaps several! All my life I shall hear his heart-rending appeal. But who could have saved him from that terrible hug? Captain Nemo nevertheless flung himself at the squid and sliced off another tentacle. The lieutenant and the crew were slashing away at other monsters who were mounting the platform on all sides. Conseil and I brought our axes down again and again into the fleshy masses. A strong smell of musk filled the air.

For a moment I thought that the poor man would be saved from the squid that held him so fiercely. Seven of its eight arms had been severed! Only one arm, brandishing the man like a feather, still waved in the air. But as the captain and his lieutenant lunged at it, the animal ejected a stream of black liquid from a sac in its abdomen. We were blinded. When the cloud had dispersed, the squid had disappeared, carrying with it my countryman!

With what a rage we threw ourselves at these monsters! Ten or twelve were now mounting the platform and we, like men possessed, rolled pell-mell into the nest of truncated tentacles as they writhed in waves of red blood and black ink. These slimy arms seemed to grow back again, like Hydra heads. I saw Ned fling his harpoon between the eyes of a monster, yet the next moment he was thrown down by another. Now the giant was opening his dread beak; in a moment he would cut Ned in two. I rushed to help him, but Captain Nemo was faster. His hatchet disappeared between the enormous jaws. Miraculously saved, Ned got up and plunged his harpoon deep into the squid's triple heart!

"I owed myself this revenge," Captain Nemo said. "Tit for tat!"

Ned bowed his head and said nothing.

The battle had lasted for fifteen minutes. Vanquished, the monsters finally left us and disappeared beneath the waves. Captain Nemo, spattered with blood, leaned against the searchlight cage, gazing over the sea that had devoured one of his companions. Great tears welled up in his eyes. It was the second man he had lost since we had come aboard, and that sailor, my compatriot, would not even sleep with his comrades in the peaceful coral cemetery!

At last Captain Nemo went into his cabin. I saw nothing of him for some time. But he was sad and irresolute; I could tell that from the way the vessel behaved, the vessel that reflected his every mood as a body reflects its soul. The *Nautilus* did not stay on any course; sometimes it floated like a corpse at the mercy of the waves and currents. Its propeller had been disentangled from the terrible beak, but it was hardly ever used.

TEN DAYS PASSED LIKE THAT. It was not until May 1 that the *Nautilus*, having sighted the Bahamas, resumed its northerly course. We were now following the largest current in the seas, the Gulf Stream. Standing on the platform with Conseil, I invited him to thrust his hand into the water. He was astonished to discover that it was neither hot nor cold.

"That's because the temperature of the Gulf Stream, as it leaves the Gulf of Mexico," I said, "is about the same as the temperature of the human body. The Gulf Stream is a vast heat distributor that allows the coasts of Europe to be decked eternally in green."

Later, at the salon window, we saw how this current carried with it all kinds of living beings: rays with long tails and bodies twenty-five feet across; dolphins and small sharks; sirens a yard long; parrot fish that rival the most beautiful tropical birds in color; little gobies with brown-spotted bellies; and, among several other remarkable species, the beautiful American horsemen, decorated with medals and ribbons.

On May 8 we were passing Cape Hatteras, at the latitude of North Carolina, where the Stream is seventy-five miles wide. The nearby shores were inhabited, and the sea was plowed incessantly by steamers. Escape should have been possible, but the weather turned stormy. It was too dangerous for a small boat, as Ned himself admitted. But he fretted more and more. "Professor," he said to me, "this has got to stop. I had enough of the South Pole, and I won't follow your Captain Nemo to the North Pole!"

"But what'll we do, Ned?" I asked.

"Remember my idea! We must talk to the captain! You said nothing when we were near your country. I want to speak up, now that we're near mine! When I think that in a few days the *Nautilus* will be in the latitude of the mouth of the Saint Lawrence, the river that flows by *my* hometown of Quebec, I could go mad. I want the captain's intentions in black and white, Professor, once for all. Speak only for me, in my name alone, if you prefer."

Obviously the Canadian was at the end of his patience. I could sense what he was suffering, for nostalgia had gripped me too. For seven months we had had no news at all from land. Besides, Captain Nemo's isolation, his taciturnity, especially since the fight with the squid, all made me see things in a different light.

"Well, Professor?" Ned prodded me.

"Ned, I see the captain so rarely now."

"All the more reason to go looking for him. Or shall I find him myself?"

"No, let me handle it. Tomorrow . . ."

"Today."

"All right, today," I said, to prevent him from making a serious blunder.

Left alone, now the decision had been made, I wanted to carry it out at once. Going to the captain's chamber, I knocked on the door. No answer. I knocked again. Then I opened the door. The captain looked up from his worktable, frowning. "What do you want? I am preoccupied with my work!"

This was not a very auspicious beginning. "Captain," I said, "I must speak to you about a matter that can't wait."

"And what could that be?" he replied sarcastically. "Have you discovered some secret of the sea that has escaped me?" We seemed far away from each other. But before I could attempt to close the gap, he showed me a manuscript on the table. "Here, Professor, is a manuscript written in several languages. Signed by me, it contains a summary of all my studies of the sea and an account of my life. With God's help, it will not perish with me! The last survivor of all of us on the *Nautilus* will toss it into the sea in an unsinkable container, and it will drift wherever the waves take it."

The name of the man! His life story written by himself! Then the mystery of Captain Nemo would someday be unveiled? But at that moment, I saw this mainly as a chance to lead up to the subject I wanted to discuss. "Captain, I can only approve of the idea that makes you take this step. But the means that you employ! Who knows what hands this container will fall into? Isn't there a better way? Couldn't you, or one of your men—"

"Never!" He cut me short.

"But I, my companions and I, we would be willing to take care of this manuscript for you, and if you would set us free—"

"Free!" He stood up.

"Yes, Captain, that is the subject I wanted to discuss. For seven months my companions and I have been on board the *Nautilus*. Is it your intention to keep us prisoners forever?"

"Professor, I will give you the same answer I gave you seven months ago. Whoever steps on board the *Nautilus* must never leave it."

"But that's slavery. And the slave has the right to seek his freedom!"

"Who has denied you that right? Have I ever chained you with an oath?"

"Captain," I said, "I'm not thinking so much of myself. For me, research is a seductive passion that can make me forget everything else. Like you, I am a man who can live ignored and obscure, with the fragile hope of someday leaving to the future the results of my work. In short, I can admire you and follow you without displeasure in a way of life which, up to a certain point, I can understand. But there are aspects of your way of life which are shrouded in mystery that my companions and I can have no part in. Whenever our hearts could beat with yours, moved by your sorrows or your acts of genius or courage, we have been obliged to keep to ourselves. This feeling, that we are strangers to whatever is important to you, makes our position impossible, even for me, and especially for Ned Land. Every man is worthy of consideration. Have you ever asked yourself how a love of liberty can give rise to thoughts of vengeance in a nature like Ned's? What it can make him think, try, risk!"

I paused. Captain Nemo got up. "Let Ned Land think, try, risk whatever he wants! What does it matter to me? I didn't go hunting for him! I didn't capture him for my own amusement! I have nothing more to say to you, Professor. This is the first time you have raised this question; let it be the last."

I left him. Our situation was serious. I told my two friends about this interview. "Now we know for sure," said Ned, "that we can expect nothing from this man. The *Nautilus* will shortly be approaching Long Island. We'll get away no matter what the weather is!"

But over the next few days the weather became more and more menacing. We saw definite indications of a hurricane. The sky became white and milky. Low clouds sped swiftly by. The swelling sea rose in long waves. The barometer dropped, and all the birds vanished, with the exception of the stormy petrel, that friend of the tempest! Then, on May 12, just as the *Nautilus* was sailing a few miles out from the entrance to the port of New York, the storm broke.

Captain Nemo, to satisfy some inexplicable whim, decided to brave it out on the surface. By three p.m. the southwesterly wind had reached fifty miles an hour! Captain Nemo had taken his place on the platform, tied around the waist to prevent his being washed overboard by the huge waves. I hoisted myself out on deck and also made myself fast, dividing my admiration between the storm and the man who could face it. The *Nautilus*, sometimes lying on its side, sometimes standing up like a mast, rolled and pitched horribly.

Near five p.m., a torrential rain fell, but it calmed neither wind nor sea. The hurricane was now blowing about a hundred miles an hour, and the raging waves now measured as much as fifty feet in height and six hundred feet in breadth. The intensity of the storm increased with night. By ten p.m. the sky was on fire. The heavens were crisscrossed with violent lightning. A terrible noise filled the air, a confused sound, compounded from the crashing of the waves, the roaring of the wind in all directions, and the clapping of the thunder. Now the drops of rain changed into sparks of fire. Was Captain Nemo courting a death worthy of himself, a death by lightning? Sparks were dancing on the steel spur of his boat as I crawled on my belly toward the hatch. I descended to the salon. It was impossible to stand up inside the ship.

Captain Nemo at last came down, near midnight. I heard the reservoirs filling, little by little, and the *Nautilus* slowly submerged. Through the salon windows I saw terrified fish pass like phantoms through the fiery sea. A few were hit by lightning, right before my eyes, struck dead!

We had to go down twenty-five fathoms, into the very bowels of the sea, before we could find repose. But down there, what tranquillity, what peace! Down there, who could say that a terrible hurricane was loose on the surface of the ocean?

XVII. A HECATOMB

THE HURRICANE HAD thrown us northeast. All hopes of escape vanished. Poor Ned, in despair, hid himself away, like Captain Nemo. But Conseil and I never left each other.

On May 15, having wandered for some days among those fogs so dreaded by mariners in the area, we were at the southern tip of the Grand Banks of Newfoundland. This bank is the product of alluvia, large heaps of organic matter, brought either from the equator by the Gulf Stream or from the North Pole by the counter-current of cold water that skirts the American coast. The depth of the sea there is no more than a few hundred fathoms. Cod abound in these waters and, as the *Nautilus* opened a path through their thick ranks, Conseil observed, "What! Those are cod! I've always believed that cod were flat, like flounder!"

"Naïve boy!" I cried. "Cod are flat only in the fish store, where they've been opened and spread out! But in the water, they're spindle shaped for fast traveling."

"If monsieur says so, I believe it. But what swarms!"

"Yes, my friend, and they would be even more numerous if it weren't for their enemies, hogfish and men! Did you know that eleven million eggs have been counted in just one female?"

"I'll trust the professor. I won't count them."

As we traveled over the bottom of the Grand Banks, it took some adroit maneuvering for the *Nautilus* to get through the underwater web of fishing lines! But at last we swerved east, to follow the "telegraphic plateau" on which the Atlantic Cable is laid.

It was on May 17, about five hundred miles out from Newfoundland and at a depth of nine thousand feet, that I first spotted the cable. Conseil at first thought it was a gigantic sea serpent and set to work to classify it. But I disabused him, and gave him some background.

The first cable had been laid in 1857–1858, but after having transmitted about four hundred messages it ceased to function. In 1863, a second attempt was made to lay a cable, but it snapped several hundred miles away from the Irish coast. Not discouraged, the audacious American promoter of the enterprise, Cyrus Field, announced a new series of bonds. They were immediately bought up, and a third cable, stronger and better insulated than the others, was embarked on the *Great Eastern* on July 13, 1866. On July 23, when the *Great Eastern* was at about our present position, she received by telegraph from Ireland the news that an armistice had been signed by Prussia and Austria after the battle of Sadowa. On July 27, in a heavy fog, she completed her crossing of the Atlantic and reached Heart's Content, her destination. The enterprise was a success. For its first message, young America sent to older Europe these sage words so rarely understood: GLORY TO GOD IN THE HIGHEST, AND PEACE ON EARTH TO MEN OF GOOD WILL.

Looking at the cable nearly two years later, Conseil and I saw that by now it had become covered with fragments of shell and encrusted with foraminifera. Protected from the motions of the sea, it was lying tranquil. The *Nautilus* followed it to its lowest point, fourteen thousand, five hundred feet down, and there it reposed without any strain.

We continued east, and then soon after that we swung south, rounding Ireland. Was Captain Nemo heading for the English Channel? Ned questioned me constantly about our course. But how would I know? We never saw Captain Nemo. On May 30 we passed between Land's End, the southern extremity of England,

and the Scilly Isles. If the captain wanted to enter the English Channel, he would now have to turn sharply to the east. He did not.

During the day of May 31, the *Nautilus* described a series of circles that greatly intrigued me. The following day, June 1, the boat continued these same circular motions. It was evidently trying to find a precise spot in the ocean. Toward noon, when I was on the platform, Captain Nemo himself came out to shoot the sun. The sea was calm, the sky was pure. Eight miles to the east, a large steamship was outlined against the horizon. It flew no flag, so I could not tell its nationality. Just before the sun reached its zenith, Captain Nemo put his sextant to his eye and peered through it with great care. The *Nautilus* lay motionless. Suddenly the captain spoke: "This is the place!"

He went down the hatch. Had he seen the ship that had changed its course and seemed to be approaching us? I could not tell. I went back to the salon. Next minute, the *Nautilus* submerged, coming to rest on the bottom at four hundred and twenty fathoms.

The lights dimmed, the starboard panel opened, and I could see the waters brilliantly illuminated. In their midst, on the bottom, a large object attracted my attention. It looked like a ruin covered with a snowlike mantle of white shells! Examining it more carefully, I could make out the encrusted form of a ship, stripped of its masts, which must have spent many years on the bottom.

Just what was this ship? Why was the *Nautilus* visiting its grave? Was there anything besides a mere shipwreck that had attracted it beneath the waves?

I didn't know what to make of it, when next to me I heard Captain Nemo saying in a slow voice, "This vessel was launched in 1762. It carried seventy-four guns, and participated in many battles. On April sixteenth, 1794, it joined at Brest the squadron of Villaret de Joyeuse, ordered by the Republic of France to escort a convoy of wheat coming from America. On the eleventh and twelfth Prairial, in year II of the Revolutionary calendar, this squadron encountered the English fleet. Professor, today is the thirteenth Prairial, June first, 1868. It is now seventy-four years, day for day, at this exact spot, latitude 47° 24' north and longitude 17° 28' west, that this ship, after a heroic fight, stripped of its three masts, one third of its crew out of action, preferred sinking with its three hundred and fifty-six men rather than surrender! Nailing their flag to the poop, they disappeared beneath the waves with the cry of 'Long live the Republic!' "

"The *Avenger!*" I exclaimed.

"Yes, Professor, the *Avenger*. What a beautiful name!"

I stared at him as he crossed his arms. The way he had pronounced those last words, with such sudden warmth—the very name of the *Avenger*, whose significance I could not escape—had a profound effect on me. Now, as he stood motionless, staring with glowing features at the glorious wreck, I realized that it was no ordinary misanthropy that had made him and his men shut themselves up inside the *Nautilus*. It was rather a hatred, which time could never weaken. But did this hatred still require revenge?

The *Nautilus* was rising slowly. A slight rolling told me when we were on the surface. Then suddenly there was a dull *boom!* I looked at the captain. He did not budge. "Captain!"

He did not answer. I climbed to the platform. Ned and Conseil were out there. "Where did that—that detonation come from?" I asked.

"That was a cannon firing," Ned replied.

I looked toward the vessel I had seen before. It was now only about six miles away. "What kind of ship is it, Ned?"

"From her rigging, and the height of her masts, I bet she's a warship. I hope she sinks this confounded *Nautilus*."

"Can you tell her nationality?" I asked.

The Canadian knit his eyebrows. "No, she's not flying any flag, only a pennant on her mainmast."

For fifteen minutes we watched the ship steaming toward us. Soon Ned could make out that she was a large two-decked armored ram. Smoke was pouring from her funnels. Her sails were furled. She still hoisted no flag, and distance made it impossible to make out the colors of her pennant.

"Professor," Ned said, "if that ship passes within a mile, I'll throw myself into the sea. I suggest you follow me."

"Monsieur will recall that we have some experience as swimmers," Conseil said. "He can count on me to tow him toward the ship."

I was about to answer when a puff of white smoke burst from the bow of the oncoming ram. Seconds later a heavy object hit the water near us, splashing the stern, and then I heard a loud explosion. "They're shooting at *us!*" I exclaimed.

"If monsieur— Whew!" Conseil was suddenly sprayed with water as another shell dropped near us. "If monsieur will permit me to say it, they are shooting at the narwhal."

"But surely they can see that men are involved!"

"Perhaps that's exactly why!" Ned said, looking directly at me.

Light burst on my consciousness. By now the whole world probably knew the truth about the "sea monster"! When Ned had hit it with his harpoon, Commander Farragut had probably recognized it as a submarine boat, more dangerous than a supernatural cetacean. Yes, that must be it! And now on every sea they were hunting down this engine of destruction.

Did Captain Nemo use the *Nautilus* for massive retaliation? That night in the Indian Ocean, when we were locked up in that cell, he must have attacked some ship! The man buried in the coral cemetery must have been a casualty of that battle! Yes, that was it! The nations of the world were no longer chasing a chimerical creature but a man with a sworn hatred for them. Instead of meeting friends on board that ship, then, we could expect only merciless enemies. Shells rattled about us. The ram was now not more than three miles away.

"A thousand devils!" Ned said. "Why don't we signal them! At least, then, they'll know there are honest men on board!" He took out his handkerchief. But he had hardly waved when, in spite of his great strength, he was knocked down on the deck.

"Miserable fool!" roared the captain. "Would you like to be pierced by the *Nautilus'* spur before I run it into that ship?"

Captain Nemo was terrible to hear, more terrible to see. His face was deathly pale and his pupils were fearfully contracted as he turned from Ned and shouted toward the armored ram: "Oh, you ship of an Evil Power! You know who I am! I don't need to see your flag to know who you are! But I will show you mine!"

Then he unfurled a black flag, similar to the one he had planted at the South Pole. A shell hit our hull obliquely, glanced past the captain and fell into the sea. He turned to me: "Go below, you and your companions! Below!"

"Captain, are you going to attack the ship?"

"I'm going to sink that ship! And I advise you not to judge me. Chance has let you see what you should not have seen. The attack has begun. The counterattack will be terrible. Go below."

"That ship, what nationality is it?"

"You don't know? So much the better. Below!"

We could only obey. About fifteen sailors stood around the captain, staring with fierce hatred at the approaching ram. The same need for revenge seemed to animate every one of them.

I was going down when another shell hit the *Nautilus*, and I heard the captain exclaim, "Shoot, mad ship! You won't escape the spur of the *Nautilus!* But I won't sink you here! I won't let your ruins mingle with the *Avenger*'s!"

I reached my cabin. The propeller was turning. The *Nautilus* was soon out of range of the ram's guns, but I gathered that the armored ship still followed.

About four p.m., unable to contain my patience, I went up the central staircase again. The captain was still pacing the platform, looking at the ship, which was now five or six miles to leeward. He was moving around it like a wild beast, attracting it eastward. Did he still hesitate to attack? I wanted to mediate once more, but as I opened my mouth he demanded silence, saying, "I am the law and I am the judge! I am the oppressed and there is the oppressor! Thanks to him, I have lost everything that I loved—my country, my wife, my children, my father, my mother! Everything I hate is out there! Don't say another word!"

I rejoined Ned and Conseil. "We've got to escape!" I said. "The ram will be sunk before morning. I don't know what nationality it is—but whatever it is, I would rather be sunk with it than become an accomplice to such an atrocity!"

"That's the way I feel too," Ned said very coolly. "But let's wait until dark."

Night came. Everything was quiet on board. We were still on the surface, rolling a bit. We decided to jump overboard as soon as the ram got close enough to see us or hear us. Several times I thought the *Nautilus* was set to attack, but Captain Nemo still contented himself with leading his enemy on and then moving swiftly away. The way I saw it, we should have to wait until the *Nautilus* attacked the ram at her waterline; then we would escape.

At three a.m., more anxious than ever, I climbed to the platform. The captain was still out there, standing near his flag, staring always at the two-decker ram. The tranquil sea offered the stars the finest mirror they would ever have in which to reflect their image. I shuddered as I compared the deep calm of nature with the passion brewing on board. The ram was about two miles away, always approaching the phosphorescence that signaled the location of the *Nautilus*. I could see its riding lights, green and white, and its lantern hanging from the mizzenmast. Its rigging was lit with a dim glow, showing that the furnaces were fired to the limit. From its funnels, red ashes and sparks rose like shooting stars.

Although I stayed there until dawn, the captain never noticed me. At the first crack of the sun's light the ram opened up with her guns. The moment could not be far off when the *Nautilus* would retaliate, and I was about to go below to alert my companions when the lieutenant mounted the platform. Several sailors followed him to "clear the deck for action," as naval men would say. First they lowered the iron railing around the platform, and then they pushed the pilot's cage and the searchlight cage down into the hull until they were flush with the deck. Now, nothing protruded from the long, steel surface of this cigar-shaped ship; there was nothing to hamper its freedom of movement.

When I returned to the salon, I could feel that the captain was reducing speed. He was letting the ram get closer! "Friends," I said, "this is it! Shake hands, and God bless you!"

Ned was resolute, Conseil calm, I so nervous I could not contain myself. We walked through the library—but as I opened the door leading to the staircase I heard the hatch close sharply. The Canadian tried to rush up the ladder, but I stopped him. A familiar hissing told us that the tanks were filling. In a few moments the *Nautilus* was fathoms below the surface. Now I could see the captain's strategy. He had decided not to strike the ram at its waterline, where it was armored, but below the waterline, underneath its metal carapace! We had lost our chance.

Taking refuge in my cabin, we stared at each other without saying a word. In this state we waited for what we knew must come. I needed every one of my senses. The *Nautilus'* speed was perceptibly increased; it was preparing to rush. Then the whole ship shuddered! I cried out. I could feel the collision, but the impact was surprisingly light. I heard rattling, scraping, as I felt the steel spur penetrating! The *Nautilus* went right through the armored ram, the way a sailmaker's needle goes through canvas!

Beside myself, I rushed hysterically into the salon. Captain Nemo, mute, somber, implacable, was staring through the port window, anxious not to miss one detail of his victim's agony. Thirty feet away I could see the hull of the sinking ram. Water was pouring through it with a noise like thunder. I could see the double row of guns. Dark shadows moved about the deck. The poor creatures were crowding the shrouds, clinging to the masts, struggling in the water. It was a human ant heap surprised by an invasion from the sea.

Paralyzed with anguish, breathless and voiceless, I was watching too as the enormous vessel slowly settled. The *Nautilus* followed her, observing every movement. Suddenly there was an explosion as the compressed air blew up the ram's decks. The *Nautilus* swerved from the shock, and the dark mass now sank rapidly and disappeared from sight, lost with all hands.

Captain Nemo, that terrible judge, that archangel of hate, was still looking. When he walked into his room I followed him with my eyes. On the far wall, near those watercolor sketches of his heroes, I saw a portrait of a young woman with two small children. The captain looked at them, stretched out his arms toward them and, kneeling down, broke into deep sobs.

XVIII. THE LAST WORDS OF CAPTAIN NEMO

THE PANELS HAD CLOSED on the frightful scene of the sunken ram, but the lights did not go on again in the salon. All was dark and still. I returned to my cabin, where Ned and Conseil had waited in silence. I felt an insurmountable revulsion for Captain Nemo. Whatever these men had done to him, he had no right to punish in this way. And he had made me, if not an accomplice, at least a witness to his vengeance. It was insufferable.

When the lights went on again, about eleven o'clock, I went back to the salon. No one was there. I studied the instruments. The *Nautilus* was heading north at twenty-five knots, five fathoms down. I could see on the chart that we were passing the mouth of the English Channel. At a frightening pace we were hurtling toward the North Sea. But where exactly would the captain flee after his horrible reprisal? Back in my cabin, I could not sleep. I was tormented with nightmares. The scene of destruction was continually in my mind's eye.

In fact, from that day on, I could not be sure what part of the North Atlantic basin we were sailing. Our bearings were no longer marked on the planisphere. I couldn't even guess at the time anymore. All clocks on board had stopped! It seemed, as in polar lands, that night and day no longer followed their regular pattern.

I can only estimate that we sailed this haphazard course for fifteen or twenty days. I don't know how much longer we would have gone on that way if it had not been for the sudden catastrophe that ended our journey. I saw nothing of Captain Nemo, or of any member of the crew except for the always silent steward who brought our meals. We sailed underwater almost continuously. When we surfaced to renew our air supply, the hatches opened and closed automatically. We were lost on a ghost ship.

I must add that the Canadian, his energy and his patience exhausted, stayed, silent, in his cabin. Afraid that he would kill himself in a fit of melancholy, Conseil watched him constantly. Then one morning, as I awoke after a morbid sleep—I can no longer give dates—I saw Ned standing over me, and I heard him saying in a low voice, "We're going to make a break for it."

I got up. "When?"

"Tonight. I caught sight of land this morning, about twenty miles to the east."

"What country?"

"I can't tell. It doesn't matter; we'll take refuge there."

"Of course, Ned, of course. We'll escape tonight even if the sea swallows us up."

"The sea is bad, the wind is violent, but twenty miles in the dinghy doesn't worry me. If I'm caught, however, I'll fight. I'll force them to kill me."

"Then we die together, Ned."

How long that day seemed, that last day on board the *Nautilus!* We avoided speaking to each other for fear we would betray ourselves in some way. Then shortly after dinner Ned came to my cabin and said, "We won't see each other again before we leave. At ten the moon will still not have risen. We'll take advantage of the dark. Come to the boat at ten. Conseil and I will be waiting for you."

Dressing in heavy sea clothing, I arranged my notes in different pockets. My heart beat with great force. I could not slow it down, no matter how I tried. Surely my perturbation would have been obvious to Captain Nemo if he could have seen me. What was he doing? Listening at his door, I could hear footsteps. Any moment I thought he would come out and ask me why I was trying to get away.

At about half past nine I stretched out on my bed to quiet my nerves. But my overexcited brain kept reviewing all my experiences on board the *Nautilus*, all my fortunes and misfortunes since my disappearance from the *Abraham Lincoln*. The events passed before my eyes like scenes in the theater. Captain Nemo grew fantastically, his features took on superhuman proportions, he was no longer my equal, he was a man of the waters, a sea genie.

Holding my head between my hands to keep it from bursting, I closed my eyes. I tried not to think anymore. The next minute I heard faint chords of organ music, a sad harmony under an indefinable melody, truly the wailing of a soul longing to break its ties with the earth. I listened with every faculty, scarcely breathing, plunged like the captain himself into that musical ecstasy which was drawing him to the limits of the world. Then I was terrified at a sudden realization. If he was at the organ, he was in the salon, which I would have to walk through. I would have a final meeting with him after all. With a gesture, a word, he could destroy me, chain me on board!

But ten was about to strike. I could not hesitate, even if Captain Nemo himself were to rise before me. Opening my door, I moved slowly along the dark passageway. I reached the door of the salon and opened it gently. The room was completely dark. Captain Nemo was at the organ, but I think he wouldn't have seen me even if the lights were on, so absorbed was he in his music.

I moved slowly; it took me at least five minutes to reach the far door that led to the library. I was opening it when a sigh from Captain Nemo nailed me to the spot. He was getting up. I could see him clearly now, for light came into the salon from the library. He came toward me, his arms folded, gliding like a specter. I could hear him sobbing, murmuring these words—"God Omnipotent! Enough! Enough!"

Was this a confession of remorse that escaped the conscience of this man?

Madly, I flung myself through the library, mounted the central stairs and crept through the hatch into the dinghy. There were Ned and Conseil! "Let's go!" I cried. "Let's go!"

"In a moment," Ned answered. Using a monkey wrench, he fastened down the plate that closed the hatch in the side of the *Nautilus*. Then he closed the corresponding opening in the dinghy. Now he was loosening the bolts that held the dinghy to its socket in the hull of the submarine.

Suddenly we heard a commotion inside. Voices answered voices with great excitement. What was the matter? Had they discovered that we were gone? I could feel Ned Land pressing a dagger into my hand. "Yes," I murmured, "we know how to die."

The Canadian had paused in his work. I could hear one word,

repeated maybe twenty times, a terrible word, which explained the commotion that was spreading on board ship. It was not we that the men were talking about. "Maelström!" they cried. "Maelström!"

Could any more frightening word have reached our ears? So we were in the dangerous waters of the Norwegian coast! Was the *Nautilus* being sucked into that whirlpool at the very moment that we were about to shove off? The tidal currents between the islands of Ferroe and Lofoten rush with irresistible violence, creating a whirlpool which no vessel ever escapes. From all points of the horizon monstrous waves converge, forming this pattern of eddies justifiably known as the "navel of the ocean." Its power extends for ten or twelve miles, dragging not only vessels but whales and polar bears down into its fierce depths.

It was to the Maelström, then, that the captain had run his ship, voluntarily or involuntarily! It was now describing a circle whose radius was diminishing bit by bit! Our dinghy, still fastened to its hull, was carried along with dizzying speed. I experienced nausea: my nerves were numb, and I was covered with cold sweat. And what a noise all around us, what a roar echoed and reechoed for miles and miles! What a crash as the waters broke on the sharp stones at the bottom! The *Nautilus* was resisting like a human being. Its steel muscles were cracking! Suddenly it stood upright!

"We've got to hold tight," Ned shouted, "and fasten the bolts again! If we stay attached to the *Nautilus*, we may still be saved. . . ." We heard a great crash, the bolts gave way, the dinghy was yanked from its socket and hurled, like a stone shot from a sling, into the midst of the whirlpool.

My head hit the iron gunwale, and with the violence of the shock I lost consciousness.

AND SO ENDED OUR VOYAGE under the sea. What happened later that night—how our boat escaped from the terrific eddies of the Maelström—I cannot really say. But when I did regain consciousness, I was lying in a fisherman's hut in the Norwegian Lofoten Islands. My two friends, safe and sound, were pressing my hands. We embraced each other with such joy!

At this moment, we cannot think of returning to France. We are forced to wait for the steamboat that runs only twice a month from these far northern parts. But, while staying with these good people who have given us shelter, I am revising once more this account of our adventures. It is exact; not one detail has been exaggerated. It is a faithful narration of that improbable expedition through a medium now inaccessible to man. But maybe someday he will find his way there!

Will the world believe my story? I can't imagine. That isn't important, after all. I now feel able to speak with authority of those seas through which, in less than ten months, I have traveled twenty thousand leagues.

But what has happened to the *Nautilus?* Did it survive the pressures and strains of the Maelström? Is Captain Nemo alive? Does he still pursue those frightful reprisals? Or was his need for vengeance satisfied at last? Will the waves someday carry to shore his own account of his life and work? Shall I ever know the real name of the man? Will we be able to ascertain his nationality from the nationality of the missing warship?

I hope so. I hope equally that his powerful ship has conquered the most terrible whirlpool in the sea and that the *Nautilus* has survived where so many have perished. If that is so, if Captain Nemo still inhabits the ocean, his adopted country, I hope the hatred has been appeased in that wild heart! I hope his continued contemplation of so many wonders will have extinguished forever his passion for vengeance. I hope that the judge in him will die, but that the philosopher in him lives on to resume his peaceful studies of the sea. If his destiny is strange, it is also sublime. Have I not known it myself? Have I not lived for ten months that extra-natural life? And to that question posed by Ecclesiastes three thousand years ago—*Who can fathom the depths of the abyss?*—only two men of all men have the right to answer:

Captain Nemo and I.

Jules Verne
(1828–1905)

Twenty Thousand Leagues Under the Sea (1870) is the seventh of the sixty-five *Voyages Extraordinaires* written by Jules Verne between 1862 and his death in 1905. Often called the creator of science fiction, Verne combined a fascination for travel and exotic locations with a love of scientific detail and mathematic regularity.

This combination of fact and romance came to Verne naturally. Born in Nantes, France, in 1828, he was the first of five children. His father, Pierre, was a lawyer who believed in the regulation of mind, body, and spirit. To further this in his children he kept a marine telescope trained on the clock of a nearby monastery, thus assuring order in daily family life and piety in daily family thoughts. As a writer, Jules Verne would question this kind of imposed authority, especially in the historical works of his later years, such as *Family Without a Name* (1897), which described the fate of a French-Canadian family after the uprising of Quebec against England in 1837, or *Foundling Mick* (1903), which concerned the British occupation of Ireland.

Verne's books are full of despots, benevolent and otherwise. Captain Nemo is one of these; totally powerful in the undersea world he created, he grants himself absolute power of life and death over those with whom he comes in contact. The sole purpose of his life is revenge, and he sees the rest of the world only in terms of how it can afford him opportunities to attain that desire. Yet he is not totally without redeeming qualities. He is a brilliant scientist, philosopher, and musician. Furthermore, the depths of Nemo's mania for revenge reflect the hugeness of his loss of wife and children. The memory of the pain of that loss is the catalyst for his remorse and repentance, and thus, in Christian terms, redemption. For, despite Jules Verne's impatience with the restrictiveness of his father's clockwork Catholicism, he kept faith with Pierre's principles. Speaking in 1901 of his forthcoming book, *The Aerial Village*, he said: "The conclusions I put forward will be those of a believer, and entirely opposed to the theories of Darwin."

This is not to imply that Jules Verne was without doubts about the validity of his father's values, at least as they applied to his, Jules's, life. From the first, Jules loved the sea and dreamed of being a seaman, despite Pierre's expressed opinion that Jules was to be a lawyer. Compared with Pierre's dry intolerance, the wildness of seagoing must have seemed attractive. Added to this was the fact that Sophie Verne, Jules's mother, came from a family of merchant seamen and sailors, with a few artists and adventurers thrown in. Also, the family home was on a Loire River island, Ile Feydeau, which was populated with fishermen and sailors spilling over from the nearby port of Nantes. In 1839, at age eleven, Jules decided to act on his dreams and ran away to be a cabin boy on the *Coralie*, a ship bound for the West Indies.

This escapade, the first of many conflicts in Jules's life created by his father's desire for order and control as opposed to his mother's legacy of adventure and invention, ended with his father winning. The boy was taken off the ship before it could leave harbor and made to promise that "from now on, I will travel only in my imagination."

Thus, until he was twenty Jules appeared to devote himself to the bourgeois existence waiting for him, as he studied law and fell in love with a respectable cousin. Then in 1848 the cousin laughed at his verses and married a rival, and his brother Paul shipped out to the West Indies as a naval apprentice. Jules began to act so badly all Nantes was gossiping, and his parents decided to send him to Paris (on a very limited allowance) to finish his legal training.

By November, Jules was settled in happily, part of the Left Bank circle of would-be writers that hovered around Alexandre Dumas. In 1850, he finished his law degree and had a play, *Broken Straws*, produced. It was successful enough to run for twelve nights, and it thoroughly shocked his father with its immorality. It was, however, good enough to make reviewers wonder if Dumas had had a hand in writing it. This backhanded praise inspired Jules to try his luck as a writer, rather than going home to Nantes and taking over the family law office. Hurt and angry, his father cut off his son's allowance, but Jules found work as a secretary to the Theatre-Lyric and began studying mathematics with a cousin, Henri Garcet. This professor would later check the accuracy of the math in the *Voyages Extraordinaires*.

By 1857, Jules was tired of the Theatre-Lyric, tired of poverty, tired of being single, and profoundly depressed by his utter lack of success as a writer. He was ready to marry and did so to the first presentable woman who would accept him. Honorine Anne Hebe Morel, née Fraysne de Viane, was a pretty, respectable, unimaginative twenty-six-year-old widow with two children. Once again Jules had opted for the regulation and order of his father's example.

Not surprisingly, the marriage was an unhappy one, producing only one son, Michel. Jules spent little time at home, preferring when he was there to be alone in his study, writing. Still, domesticity seemed to provide the background that Jules needed in order to produce. Before his marriage, his brother-in-law had helped him buy a seat on the stock exchange, and he began getting up at 5:00 A.M. to give himself a few hours to read and write before going to his job. Verne began a period of feverish work that would lay the foundation for the next thirty-five years. He took notes on everything he read, being especially fond of magazines like *Musée des Familles*, a *National Geographic* type of publication that in the 1850s carried articles on such subjects as atmospheric electricity, sea serpents, India, Turkey, and mining, as well as short stories and verses (some contributed by Verne). The notes he took went into pigeonholes in his study and were later used for reference and factual detail in his writing. By 1895, he was estimated to have over 25,000 of these note cards, all of which he destroyed before his death.

In 1862 Verne's hard work paid off when the publisher Hetzel asked him to sign a contract for two books a year because of a new work of Verne's, *Five Weeks in a Balloon*. In this story Verne for the first time struck the balance of factual detail and romantic adventure that was to prove so hugely popular. It is his reputation for scientific accuracy that has earned him the title of Father of Science Fiction, yet many of his books, like *Five Weeks in a Balloon*, are really pure adventure stories, with none of the fantastic technology we associate with science fiction today. Jules Verne was first of all a romantic writer, in the tradition of Edgar Allan Poe, James Fenimore Cooper, and Sir Walter Scott. He loved glamorous locations—the Scottish Highlands, the Norwegian fjords, the Canadian wilderness. If he set some of his novels on comets or on the moon, it was no more than an extension of his fascination with faraway places. But it is true that the quality of his interest in exotic locales differentiates him from the purely romantic writers. For Jules Verne, mood and atmosphere meant nothing without facts and measurements. For him, everything had to be grounded in the possible. And out of the true, the real, and the exact, he was able to imagine the wonderful and the fantastic, and make it believable. As he said to a reporter who asked him for his thoughts on H. G. Wells (another father of science fiction):

> I make use of physics. He invents. I go to the moon in a cannon ball, discharged from a cannon. Here there is no invention. He goes to Mars in an airship, that does away with the law of gravitation. . . . Show me this metal. Let him produce it.

It was this quality, of taking what was already known and proved and extrapolating from it, that made Verne's work so fascinating to a nineteenth century caught up in the romance of exploration. New continents, new technology, new worlds—there seemed to be no limits to the uses that man could find for science and machines. And for Jules Verne himself, science fiction gave him a way to resolve the conflict he struggled with all his life. For here was mathematical detail, the necessity for regulation and order, but all in the service of exploring the unknown.

Other Titles by Jules Verne

Around the World in Eighty Days. George M. Towle, translator. New York: Bantam, 1984.
At the North Pole: The Adventures of Captain Hatteras. London: Amereon, 1976.
Desert of Ice. London: Amereon, 1976.
Five Weeks in a Balloon. London: Amereon, 1976.
From the Earth to the Moon. New York: Airmont.
Journey to the Center of the Earth. Morristown, NJ: Silver Burdett, 1985.
The Mysterious Island. Isaac Asimov, editor. New York: New American Library, 1986.
Works of Jules Verne. New York: Outlet, 1986.